P9-DGH-307

WEEKLY READER CHILDREN'S BOOK CLUB
INTERMEDIATE DIVISION

EDDIE'S GREEN THUMB

By the Same Author

Published by William Morrow and Company

HERE COMES THE BUS! 1963
SNOWBOUND WITH BETSY. 1962
ANNIE PAT AND EDDIE. 1960
EDDIE AND LOUELLA. 1959
BETSY'S WINTERHOUSE. 1958
EDDIE MAKES MUSIC. 1957
BETSY'S BUSY SUMMER. 1956
EDDIE AND HIS BIG DEALS. 1955
BETSY AND THE CIRCUS. 1954
EDDIE'S PAY DIRT. 1953
THE MIXED-UP TWINS. 1952
EDDIE AND GARDENIA. 1951
BETSY'S LITTLE STAR. 1950
EDDIE AND THE FIRE ENGINE. 1949
PENNY GOES TO CAMP. 1948
LITTLE EDDIE. 1947

Published by Harcourt, Brace and World

PENNY AND PETER. 1946
BETSY AND THE BOYS. 1945
HERE'S A PENNY. 1944
BACK TO SCHOOL WITH BETSY. 1943
PRIMROSE DAY. 1942
BETSY AND BILLY. 1941
TWO AND TWO ARE FOUR. 1940
"B" IS FOR BETSY. 1939

WEEKLY READER CHILDREN'S BOOK CLUB

Presents

EDDIE'S GREEN THUMB

written and illustrated by
CAROLYN HAYWOOD

William Morrow and Company
New York 1964

Alan N. Houghton Library
Renbrook School
2865 Albany Avenue
West Hartford, CT 06117

9147

83-323

Copyright © 1964 by Carolyn Haywood

All rights reserved.
Published simultaneously in the Dominion of
Canada by George J. McLeod Limited, Toronto.
Printed in the United States of America.

Library of Congress Catalog Card Number 64-18998

Weekly Reader Book Club Edition

To

my young friends, the Shepards:

Ruth,

Dwight, and

"Trip" (I.M. III)

CONTENTS

1. Anna Patricia's Seed Project 13
2. Rabbits in the Garden 33
3. I Hate Turnips 52
4. Sidney Gets a Crow 68
5. Eddie Goes to a Bazaar 85
6. Trouble in the Gardens 106
7. How Does His Garden Grow? 123
8. The Vegetable Stand 142
9. Eddie's Green Thumb 162

EDDIE'S GREEN THUMB

Chapter One

ANNA PATRICIA'S SEED PROJECT

EDDIE WILSON sat down to Sunday dinner. He looked at his father at the head of the table. He was busy slicing a baked ham. It smelled good. He looked at his mother sitting opposite his father and winked his eye at her. She winked back.

"I saw you wink," said his oldest brother, Rudy.

"No, you didn't," said Eddie.

"I did so," said Rudy. "You screw your face all up when you wink."

The twins, Joe and Frank, shouted with laughter. Joe, who was sitting beside Rudy, said, "Eddie's going to tell us one of his big ideas, bet you anything!"

"Eddie's all puffed up like a balloon," said Frank. "He always looks that way when he thinks he has something important to tell."

Eddie just grinned. "This is going to be good!" said Rudy.

"It's going to be crazy," said Joe.

"Guess he's found a new junkyard," said Frank. "You know how Eddie loves junk!"

Eddie's mother spoke up. "Now, boys," she said, "stop this nonsense. Let Eddie tell us what it is."

"Well," said Eddie, "we have a new project at school, only we're not going to do it in school."

"What kind of a project?" said Joe.

"It's a Green Thumb project," said Eddie.

"Who ever heard of a green thumb?" said Rudy.

"Isn't that just like Eddie," said Frank. "He gets all excited over a green thumb."

"Just like Little Jack Horner," said Joe. "He stuck in his thumb and pulled out a plum. What are you going to stick your thumb into, Eddie?"

"Is the prize a green thumb?" asked Frank. "What do you do with it?"

"Use it for a paperweight, I guess," said Rudy.

"No, you suck it!" said Joe.

"That's right!" cried Frank. "A green thumb all-day sucker."

"Lime or spearmint, Eddie?" asked Rudy.

"Dad!" Eddie cried. "Make them stop. How can I tell you about the project with all this racket?"

Mr. Wilson handed a plate to Eddie. "Boys," he said, "stop the racket and let Eddie tell about the project." Eddie's brothers quieted.

"Now, Eddie," said his mother, "tell us about the green thumb."

"You see," said Eddie, "we're all going to have gardens and grow things."

"You mean flowers?" said Rudy.

"No, vegetables," said Eddie.

"Where does the green thumb come in?" Rudy asked.

"Well," said Eddie, feeling important because he knew something his brothers didn't know. "When you're a good gardener, like I'm going to be, you have a green thumb."

"You mean it won't wash off?" said Frank.

"Silly," said Eddie. "You don't really have it. When somebody is awful cocky, you say he has a swelled head. It doesn't show on his head, does it?"

"Oh, like having a sweet tooth when you like candy and cookies," said Joe.

"Sure," Eddie replied.

"Where are you going to have your garden?" Rudy asked.

"Out in the backyard, of course," replied Eddie.

"Eddie," said his father, "that is the best idea you have ever come up with since you were born. Think of the money I'll save!"

"And think of the fresh vegetables we'll have," said Mrs. Wilson. "What are you going to plant in your garden?"

"Oh, all sorts of things," said Eddie. "Carrots and radishes, onions and beans and tomatoes, and watermelons, of course, because I love watermelons."

"And pumpkins?" Joe asked. "Don't forget pumpkin pie."

"Sure, pumpkins," said Eddie.

"How about corn?" asked Rudy.

"Yep, corn," said Eddie, "and lettuce and cucumbers."

"And cabbage?" said Frank.

"No cabbage!" said Eddie. "I hate cabbage!"

"This sounds like a very big project," said Mr. Wilson. "Sounds more like a farm than a garden."

"Don't you think it's a swell project?" Eddie asked.

"I think it will be fine," his father replied, "if our yard is big enough to hold all those vegetables."

"Don't forget, I have to have room for my flower garden," said his mother. "I don't want corn and watermelons in with my petunias."

"I won't get into your petunias, Mum," said Eddie. "You just show me where I can have my garden, and I'll raise the best vegetables you ever saw."

"Dad," said Joe, winking at his father, "you'll have to buy a plow for Eddie now."

"And a horse to pull the plow," said Frank.

"Oh, no!" said Rudy. "Eddie will have to have a tractor." Everyone laughed.

"Annie Pat is going to have a garden in her yard, too," said Eddie. Anna Patricia Wallace was in Eddie's class, and they were very good friends.

"Bet she'll plant everything upside down," said Rudy.

"I guess she will," said Eddie, " 'cause Annie Pat makes some awful messes." Everyone laughed. "But you know what?" Eddie continued. "They'll all come up right side up for Annie Pat."

After dinner Eddie said to his mother, "Mum, is it all right if I go over to Annie Pat's? She got a new bike yesterday, and I want to see it."

"Yes, you can go, Eddie," his mother replied. "Come back by five o'clock."

Eddie ran off. He jumped on his bicycle and pedaled over to Anna Patricia's. He rang the front doorbell and waited. In a moment the door opened. "Hi, Eddie," said Anna Patricia. "Come on in."

"I came over to see your new bike," said Eddie.

"Oh, sure! It's out in the garage," said Anna Patricia. "I'll take you to see it."

Eddie followed Anna Patricia to the garage. He looked the bicycle over carefully. "It's swell, Annie Pat," he said. "Let's go for a ride."

"Oh, I can't now," said Anna Patricia. "I'm busy. I'm working on a project out on the sun porch."

"What are you doing?" said Eddie.

Eddie followed Anna Patricia into the sun porch. A newspaper was spread on the floor. Laid out in a row on the newspaper were packages of seeds. Anna Patricia waved her hand, and said, "I'm in the seed business. I'm going to sell vegetable seeds."

"How?" said Eddie.

Anna Patricia picked up a yellow package. "My father got these big packages of seeds. I'm going to divide them into little packages, and sell them at school to everybody who is going to have a garden." Anna Patricia handed Eddie a small envelope. "I'll use these for the small packages."

"That's a swell idea, Annie Pat," said Eddie. "How about letting me come into the business with you? We'll be partners. How about it?"

Anna Patricia thought this over. Finally she said, "We can only be partners if you give me some money. You'll have to give me half of what I gave my father for these packages of seeds."

"How much did they cost?" Eddie asked.

"They cost $6.50," said Anna Patricia.

"Well," said Eddie. "I can give you half of that. Then we'll be partners."

"O.K.," said Anna Patricia. "Where's the money?"

"Oh, I don't have it with me now," said Eddie. "I don't carry that much money around with me. But I'll give it to you out of my bank. I've got it, don't worry."

"Well, bring it to school tomorrow," said Anna Patricia.

"Sure," said Eddie. "Are we partners?"

"Yes, we're partners," said Anna Patricia. "Now you can help me put these seeds into these little bags. I'll get you a teaspoon. You take a teaspoonful out of the big bag and put it into the little bag." Anna Patricia went to the kitchen and came back with a teaspoon.

She handed it to Eddie, and said, "I'm working on carrots."

"What else have you got here?" said Eddie, kneeling down beside Anna Patricia.

"Oh, all kinds of things," Anna Patricia replied.

Eddie looked over the envelopes of seeds and read them off. There were radishes, string beans, peas, cabbage, lettuce, green peppers, parsley, and squash.

"I'm going to plant sweet pickles in my garden," said Anna Patricia. "Daddy didn't get me any sweet pickles. I guess he forgot. I just love sweet pickles."

"Annie Pat!" cried Eddie. "Sweet pickles don't grow."

"Of course they grow," said Anna Patricia. "Sweet potatoes grow, don't they?"

"Sure, sweet potatoes grow," said Eddie. "But pickles are cucumbers. When you pickle cucumbers you get pickles. Anybody knows that!"

"When you pickle cucumbers, you get pickled cucumbers," said Anna Patricia. "When you pickle onions, you get pickled onions. You don't get pickles. No one would pass an onion to you and say, 'Here, have a pickle.' "

"Annie Pat," said Eddie, as he poured some beet seeds into a little bag, "you sure can get things mixed up. You get 'em so mixed up, I get mixed up. I guess if somebody handed me a carrot right now, I'd say, 'Thanks for the pickle.' "

Anna Patricia looked up from her work, and said, "The trouble with you, Eddie Wilson, is that you don't reason. You must learn to reason."

"Well, I know what a pickle is," said Eddie. "It's a cucumber."

"Oh, Eddie!" cried Anna Patricia. "I forgot to tell you, you must be careful to write the name of the seeds on the outside of each little bag. Don't get them mixed up. We don't want somebody to plant lettuce and have beans come up."

"Oh, no," said Eddie. "But I guess if you plant cucumbers, sweet pickles will come up, and you'll have the only sweet-pickle bush in the whole world." Anna Patricia smiled.

Eddie and Anna Patricia worked all afternoon packaging their seeds. When they had

finished, they had forty-two little bags. Each one was sealed and marked. Anna Patricia packed them into a shoe box, and said, "Now, when we sell these, we'll make a lot of money."

"Let's see how much we'll make when we sell them," said Eddie. He took a pencil from his pocket and set to work on the edge of the newspaper. "How much are we going to charge for one of these little bags?" he asked.

"Twenty cents apiece," said Anna Patricia.

Eddie wrote down on the paper, 20. Under it he wrote 42. Anna Patricia stood by, watching him. "It's much easier if you put the 42 on top and the 20 underneath," she said.

"It's all the same," said Eddie. "Don't try to mix me up."

"I do not mix things up, Eddie Wilson," said Anna Patricia. "I reason."

"Be quiet, Annie Pat!" said Eddie. "I have to multiply." Then he sat back on his heels, and said, "That comes to $8.40!"

"Oh, that's good!" cried Anna Patricia. "Course you have to subtract the $6.50 the seeds cost us from $8.40. Then we'll know how much we will make."

"Oh, I forgot that," said Eddie. He set to

work again. He wrote down on the edge of the paper $8.40, and under it he put $6.50, and got the answer, $1.90. "Well, that's not so much," he said.

"I think it's a lot," said Anna Patricia. "If you hadn't come over to my house, you wouldn't have made a single penny. You haven't even given me your $3.25."

"Well, we haven't sold 'em yet," said Eddie. "My grandmother always says, 'Don't count your chickens before they're hatched.' "

"Oh, everybody will want to buy them when we take them to school tomorrow. They'll be crazy about them. They won't have to go to the store. And my father says these are cheaper than the packages in the store, too."

"I guess they'll buy them then," said Eddie.

"I think $1.90 is good," said Anna Patricia. "I'll bet nobody else in the Library Club will make that much."

Eddie wondered what the Library Club had to do with it, but he didn't bother to ask. Eddie was used to having Anna Patricia's mind jump around. It was just like her to start talking about Library Club when he was thinking about seeds and money. "Well," said Eddie, as he said good-bye to Anna Patricia, "I'll see you in school tomorrow. Don't forget to bring the box of seeds."

"I won't forget," replied Anna Patricia.

The following morning Anna Patricia came into school with the box of seed packages. She showed them to Mrs. Bolling, the teacher, and said, "Eddie Wilson and I are partners, and we are selling seeds for the vegetable gardens."

"Yes," said Eddie, "and we hope that everybody will buy seeds from us. They don't cost as much as they do in the stores."

"Let's see them," said Sidney, who sat in the front row. Anna Patricia held up one of the little envelopes. "Don't they have pictures?" asked Sidney. "You have to have pictures."

"You won't know what is planted," said red-haired Alex.

"No, you won't," said Mary Jane, from the back of the room. "After you plant the seeds you have to put the envelope on a stick. Then you poke the stick in the ground so you can see the picture."

"Isn't anybody going to buy any of our seeds?" asked Eddie.

A chorus of voices replied, "Not without pictures."

"Very well," said Mrs. Bolling. "During art period, you can draw pictures on the envelopes." Eddie and Anna Patricia felt better.

When the art period arrived, the whole class took out their crayons. Mrs. Bolling had drawn every kind of vegetable on the blackboard. Sidney raised her hand. Mrs. Bolling said, "Yes, Sidney?"

"I can't make a picture on my envelope because it has writing on it," said Sidney. "It says *String Beans.*"

"Neither can I!" said most of the children.

"Just erase the writing," said Mrs. Bolling, "but don't forget what it says. We don't want to make any mistakes. Be sure your picture tells what is in the envelope."

"Mrs. Bolling," said Eddie, "will you please draw a watermelon on the blackboard?" Mrs. Bolling drew a watermelon.

The children drew pictures of carrots and radishes, beans and peas, cucumbers and beets, peppers and lettuce, turnips and squash. By

the end of the art period, each envelope had a picture on the outside. "Now everybody can buy their seeds," said Eddie, with a sigh of relief.

"Yes," said Anna Patricia, "and when we sell all of them, we're going to give the money we make to the Library Club project, aren't we, Eddie?"

"Huh?" said Eddie. "What do you mean, Library Club project? I thought we were having a vegetable garden project."

"Why, Eddie!" said Anna Patricia. "Everybody in the Library Club is doing something to raise money to buy more books for the library. I thought you knew. You said you wanted to be my partner."

"I missed the meeting of the Library Club the other day," said Eddie. "I didn't know about the project."

"But you do want to give the money to the Library Club, don't you?" asked Anna Patricia.

"Well, sure. But what about my $3.25?" said Eddie.

"You've got your $3.25, 'cause you didn't

give it to me," said Anna Patricia. "Eddie, you should learn to reason."

"Well, I'm glad I have something," said Eddie. "I didn't know I was working on a Library Club project. I thought I was working on a Green Thumb project. Well, I sure am glad I like books!"

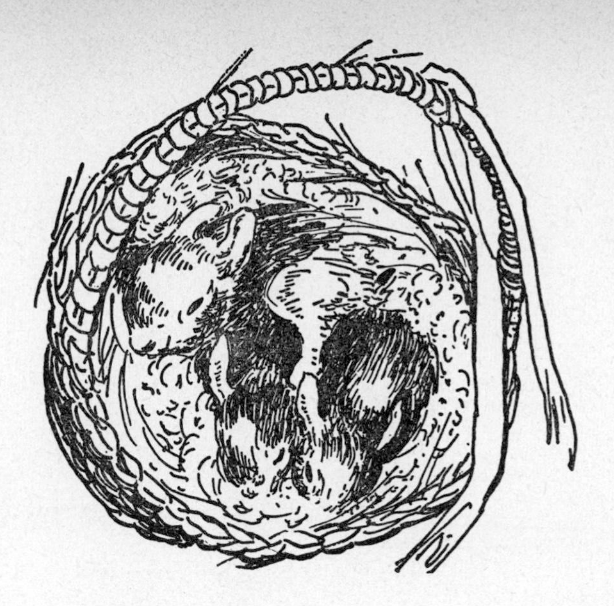

Chapter Two

RABBITS IN THE GARDEN

WHEN EDDIE woke up the next Saturday morning, the sun was shining. A soft wind was blowing. It was a perfect spring day. Right after breakfast Eddie went outside. He had the spade, the hoe, the rake, and the packages of seeds. This was the day he was going to plant his garden.

Eddie's mother showed him where he could have the garden. It was nice and open, where there would be plenty of sunshine and air.

"The hose will reach to your garden when you have to water the plants," his mother said.

"That's good," said Eddie. "I'm glad I won't have to carry the water in a watering can."

Eddie's father came out and looked over the piece of ground. "Eddie," he said, "I don't think you can dig deep enough to turn over this ground."

"Oh, yes, I can do it," said Eddie. "I'm strong as anything."

"Well, you had better let me go around the edges. Then you can keep inside the boundaries," said his father.

"Maybe that's a good idea," said Eddie.

"You will have to get those rocks out of the ground," said his father, pointing to a group of rocks. "They must be all that is left of an old stone wall. I have always meant to get rid of them."

Just then Eddie's friend Boodles came up the driveway on his bicycle. "Hi, Eddie!" he called out. "What are you doing?"

"I'm starting to dig my garden," replied Eddie.

"Oh, I've got mine all dug," said Boodles. "All my seeds planted, too."

"You're fast!" said Eddie.

Boodles parked his bike beside the garage and came over to Eddie. "Yep, I'm a quickie," he said. "Spinach is coming up already."

"You're kidding," said Eddie.

"It's the truth," said Boodles. "I put it in last Saturday. It's called quick-growing spinach. Boy! Do I have a green thumb!"

"Well, you can quick help me get these stones out of here," said Eddie.

"O.K.," said Boodles.

Eddie and Boodles walked over to the pile of stones. "These are awful old stones," said Eddie. "Dad says he guesses they are all that's left of an old stone wall."

"Guess it's from pioneer days," said Boodles.

"Maybe," said Eddie. "I remember when we were little kids, Mom and Dad used to hide our Easter baskets around these old stones." Eddie leaned down to look into an opening between two stones. What he saw made him jump. "Hot diggety!" he said softly. "There's something here."

"What is it?" asked Boodles.

Eddie knelt down and Boodles squatted beside him. "It looks like an old beat-up Easter basket," said Eddie. "But look what's in it!"

Boodles leaned over and let out a low whistle. Then, in a whisper, he said, "They're baby rabbits, three of them."

"Sure as shootin'," said Eddie. "I'll bet they belong to that cute little rabbit that's been hopping around here lately. Rudy named it Maudie. Rudy loves rabbits. He knows all about them."

Boodles put out his finger to touch one of the tiny creatures, but Eddie held him back. "Oh, you mustn't touch them," said Eddie. "Rudy says if humans touch the babies, the mother won't have anything to do with them."

"Are you sure?" said Boodles.

"Sure," said Eddie. "I know."

Suddenly Mr. Wilson called out, "Say, you fellows! Are you ever going to get those stones out of there?"

"Dad, we can't," Eddie called back. "We've got rabbits!"

"Bunnies!" Boodles said.

Mr. Wilson walked over to the boys. "See," said Eddie, pointing to the nest.

"Well, what do you know!" exclaimed Eddie's father. "Real Easter bunnies!"

"In an Easter basket!" Eddie laughed.

"That old basket looks as though it has been here for years," said Mr. Wilson.

Just then the twins came up. "What's the big show?" asked Frank.

They looked. "Boy," said Joe, "have you got trouble! Rabbits in your garden before you even get the garden laid out!"

"It'll be a cafeteria for those rabbits," said Frank. "They'll think they own the place."

"They'll probably sell your lettuce to their friends," said Joe. "You'll be raising rabbits instead of vegetables."

"I don't care," said Eddie. "They're my rabbits, and I think they're cute. I never saw such tiny ones before."

"They must have been born quite recently," said his father.

"Where do you suppose the mother got all that wool from to make the nest?" asked Boodles.

"It's her own fur," said Mr. Wilson. "She

pulled it out to make a soft nest for the babies."

"I wonder where the mother is," said Eddie. "I wonder if they belong to Maudie."

"There's one thing sure, she won't come back as long as we hang around here," said Mr. Wilson. "Eddie, you can't dig your garden today. It will be weeks before these rabbits can leave this nest."

"That's going to be awful late," said Boodles. "My spinach is already up."

"Well, you can have your spinach!" said Eddie. "I've got rabbits and nobody is going to hurt them, if I never have spinach. I don't like spinach anyway."

The group broke up. Mr. Wilson and Eddie carried the tools to the garage. Boodles said, "So long, Eddie."

As Boodles mounted his bicycle, Eddie called, "So long, Boodles!" Eddie left his father in the garage and ran to the back door. He burst into the kitchen, and shouted, "Mum! We've got baby rabbits! They're the tiniest things you ever saw! I'm going to get Dad's binoculars and watch out my window to see the mother when she comes back to feed them."

Eddie lost no time in getting settled on his windowsill, with his father's binoculars fastened on the spot where the nest of rabbits lay. He was sure that the mother would be back soon.

Sometime later his father came into the room, and said, "Any news?"

"She hasn't come back yet," Eddie replied.

His father looked at his watch. "It's getting on to lunchtime," he said. "She can't leave them too long. They should be nursed."

"Oh, Dad," said Eddie, "you don't think she is staying away because we found the babies, do you? We just looked at them. We didn't touch them."

"Oh, I'm sure we didn't do anything that would keep the mother away. It is strange, though, that she hasn't come back," said Mr. Wilson, leaving the room.

In a few minutes Rudy came in. "The twins told me about the rabbits," he said. "They may belong to Maudie. She's been looking fat."

"Well, she hasn't come back to them," said Eddie.

"You didn't poke into the nest, did you?" Rudy asked.

"Honest, Rudy! We didn't touch 'em," Eddie replied.

"Maybe she came and you didn't see her," said Rudy.

"I couldn't have missed her," said Eddie. "I've been sitting right here with these glasses so long my arms are tired."

"You sure you're looking at the right spot?" said Rudy.

"Sure!" Eddie replied. "I know exactly where it is. Didn't I find it?"

"She'd better come back soon," said Rudy.

"You don't think anything has happened to her, do you, Rudy?" said Eddie, without taking his eyes from the binoculars.

"Well, rabbits are very fast," said Rudy. "They can get away from almost anything, and no one around here would shoot a rabbit. Of course, once in a while a dog gets a rabbit."

"But you think she's all right, don't you, Rudy?" said Eddie, sounding worried.

"Oh, sure," Rudy replied.

Then Eddie, almost ready to cry, shouted, "Well, then! Why doesn't she come?"

Rudy didn't know the answer. He left Eddie, still looking out of the window, went downstairs, and put on his coat. He had decided to go out and look around. Perhaps something had happened to little Maudie. He didn't know why he felt so sure the baby rabbits were Maudie's. After all, there were lots of rabbits around.

Rudy wandered around the outside of the house, hoping to see a rabbit scamper away. There wasn't a rabbit in sight. He walked out to the pavement and crossed the street. There was a vacant lot opposite the Wilsons' house where the boys played ball. Rudy looked around the lot, still hoping to see a rabbit. He had often seen one sit still as a stone, only its whiskers trembling, as he watched it. He went quietly. He had not gone very far when he suddenly knew that he had found what he was looking for. The slight worry that he had felt suddenly became a big lump in his throat. There at his feet was a rabbit. It was as still as a stone, but it was not sitting up with quivering whiskers. It was lying on its side.

Rudy leaned over it. He saw at once that a dog had killed it, and he seemed to know, too, that it was the mother of the baby rabbits. It was the rabbit that Eddie was patiently waiting for. This was the reason she had not returned to feed her babies. As Rudy looked at her, he was sure it was Maudie.

When Rudy returned to the house, his mother was peeling potatoes. She looked up when the back door opened. Rudy's face told her that something was wrong. "What's the matter, Rudy?" she asked.

"Is Eddie still upstairs?" he asked.

"Yes," replied his mother. "He's still watching for the mother rabbit to return to those little ones."

"Well, he can stop," said Rudy. "She isn't coming back."

"How do you know?" his mother asked.

Rudy turned away, but his mother saw him brush a tear from his eye. "A dog got it. I found it over on the lot and picked it up. I'm sure it was the one that's been hopping around here. Such a tame little rabbit. I carried it over to the oak tree, and I dug a hole and buried it."

"Well, you did just the right thing, dear,"

said his mother. "Now you'll have to tell Eddie."

Eddie was still sitting on the windowsill when Rudy came back into the room. "That you, Rudy?" asked Eddie, without looking around.

"Yep," replied Rudy.

"That rabbit hasn't come back yet," said Eddie.

Rudy stood beside Eddie for a moment. Then he said, "Eddie, she isn't coming back."

"What makes you think that?" asked Eddie. For the first time since he had sat down on the windowsill, he put down the binoculars. "What makes you think that?" he repeated.

Then Rudy told Eddie how he had found the rabbit. Eddie could not hold back the tears. They rolled down his cheeks. As he brushed them away, he said, "Oh, Rudy, we've got to take care of those bunnies. I'll bet anything they are Maudie's! The poor little things, waiting out there for their mother to come back! They must be awful hungry."

"We'll go get them," said Rudy.

Eddie followed Rudy downstairs. They went outside and ran to the old stones. Rudy picked up the Easter basket very carefully. Then he carried it back to the kitchen. He placed the nest on a newspaper on the kitchen counter. His mother looked at the baby rabbits, and said, "Oh, they are very young!"

"Do we give them milk?" asked Eddie, opening the refrigerator door. "We have to hurry. They're probably starving."

"We'll never be able to make them take milk from a spoon," said Rudy. "They are too young."

"We should have a nursing bottle," said Eddie. Then he shouted, "I've got it! Sidney has a doll's nursing bottle. I know she has. I've seen it. I bet she'll lend it to me." Eddie was out the door in a flash. As he went through the hedge that separated the driveways, he was shouting, "Hey, Sid! Sid!"

Sidney opened the back door and Eddie practically fell into the Stewarts' kitchen. "Where's the fire?" asked Sidney.

"We've got baby rabbits!" said Eddie. "Little tiny bunnies! A dog got the mother, and we have to feed the babies, and I need your doll's nursing bottle. Will you lend it to me, Sid, please?"

"Sure!" said Sidney. "You wait and I'll get it." She was back in a minute with the little bottle. "Mommy," she said to her mother, "can I go see the bunnies?"

"Not now, Sidney," her mother replied, "we are ready to sit down to lunch."

"Thanks, Sid," said Eddie. "You come see 'em after you have your lunch."

"Can I feed them?" asked Sidney. "I never fed anything real with my doll's bottle."

"Sure, you can feed them," said Eddie as he ran off.

Back in his own kitchen, Rudy was looking at the little rabbits. "I've got the bottle!" said Eddie.

"I'll fill it," said Rudy. "I can do it carefully, with this little funnel."

Eddie watched his brother fill the bottle. He watched while Rudy ran hot water over it. "This will take the chill off the milk," said Rudy.

Rudy handed the bottle to Eddie, and Eddie said, "Rudy, do you think it really was the mother?"

"I'm sure it was," Rudy replied.

"Maybe you would like to feed them, 'cause

you know so much about rabbits," said Eddie.

"Thanks," said Rudy, taking the bottle out of Eddie's hand. Rudy's face was very solemn as he leaned over the nest. Then as Eddie watched he saw Rudy smile.

"Is it taking the milk?" Eddie whispered.

"Yes," said Rudy. "Boy, are they cute little things!"

"I guess we'll have to feed them during the night," said Eddie.

"Every couple of hours," said Rudy. "We'll have to set the alarm."

That night Eddie went to bed in Rudy's room. The nest of rabbits was on a chair between the two beds. When the boys were both under their covers, Eddie called very softly, "Rudy, are you awake?"

"Yep," said Rudy.

"Do you know that the mother rabbit got all of that soft wool that is in the nest out of her own fur? She pulled it right out, just to make that nest for those babies."

"I know," said Rudy. "I read a book about rabbits."

"Mothers are pretty swell, aren't they?" said Eddie.

"Sure are," said Rudy.

Rudy put the little bottle of milk under his pillow, to keep it warm. Every two hours he woke up and set the alarm again. It never woke Eddie, but Rudy fed the rabbits with the warm milk.

9147

Chapter Three

I HATE TURNIPS

DURING THE following week, between feeding the baby rabbits, Eddie got his garden dug. He found out that it took a lot of strength to turn up the hard ground, but his brother Rudy came to his help. By Saturday Eddie had planted all of his seeds. He was careful to plant them in straight rows. In the back of the garden he planted his watermelon patch. "I'm looking forward to my watermelons," Eddie said to his brother. Eddie took care to stick the empty seed envelopes into the ground, so that he would know where everything was planted.

Alan N. Houghton Library
Renbrook School
2865 Albany Avenue
West Hartford, CT 06117

83-373

After Eddie planted his seeds, he could hardly wait for them to come up. Every day, when he came home from school, he ran to see if anything green was showing above ground. His friend Boodles kept talking about his quick-growing spinach. To hear him talk you would have thought the spinach was ready to cut. Eddie began to wish that he had planted some quick-growing spinach too. It would have been something to talk about.

Eddie did a good bit of talking, however, even though he was not growing spinach. He had the rabbits to talk about. All three rabbits were growing stronger every day.

Soon Eddie's garden began to show signs of green. One day he said to Boodles, "My seeds are coming up!"

"You should see my spinach," Boodles replied.

"Don't you have anything in your garden but spinach?" asked Eddie.

"Sure," said Boodles. "Everything is coming up. It looks great!"

It wasn't long before Eddie could say to Boodles, "Everything is coming up in my garden, too. You should see my turnips."

"My carrots are as high as anything," Boodles replied. "I didn't plant any turnips. I don't like turnips."

"Well, I didn't plant any carrots 'cause I don't like carrots," said Eddie, "but I sure do like turnips!"

One day Boodles came over to Eddie's house to see the rabbits. They were growing fast, and no longer took their food from the doll's nursing bottle. Eddie was feeding them vegetables now. They liked vegetables. "Soon I'll have to build a hutch for these rabbits," said Eddie.

"I didn't know wild rabbits could be so tame," said Boodles.

After the boys had looked at the rabbits, Eddie took Boodles to see his garden. "You're not very far along," said Boodles. "Of course, you planted late." Boodles leaned over and looked at the envelope with the picture of a big turnip on it. Then he stooped down and looked at the little plants that were coming up. Boodles straightened up, and said, "Do you know what?"

"What?" said Eddie.

"Those aren't turnips. They're carrots," said Boodles.

"They are not carrots," replied Eddie. "That picture on the stick is a picture of a turnip. Anybody can tell that's a turnip!"

"Well, the picture is a turnip," said Boodles, "but what's coming up are carrots."

Just then Anna Patricia arrived on her new bicycle. She parked it by the garage and walked over to the two boys. "Hi," she said.

"Hey, Annie Pat!" said Eddie. "Boodles says these are carrots coming up here where I planted turnips."

"Well, don't be silly," said Anna Patricia. "If you planted turnips, they're turnips. You can't plant turnips and get carrots. Just a little reason tells you that."

"But maybe the envelope was wrong," said Boodles. "What if it had the wrong picture on it?"

"Don't be silly," said Anna Patricia. "You get what the picture shows."

"Well, that picture right there," said Eddie, pointing to the envelope, "is a turnip. Anybody can tell it's a turnip."

Anna Patricia leaned over and pointed to

the envelope. "Do you mean this one?" she asked.

"Sure! That one," said Eddie.

"Oh, Eddie!" said Anna Patricia. "That isn't a turnip. That's a radish!"

"A radish!" said Eddie.

"Yes," said Anna Patricia. "You've got radishes coming up here."

"How can they be radishes when they are carrots?" asked Boodles.

"Well, if they are carrots," said Anna Patricia, "why is there a picture of a radish?"

"They're turnips!" said Eddie. "I'll prove it to you!" He stooped down and very carefully pulled up one of the little plants. The three children put their heads together. They looked at the tiny root. It was round and white with a thin thread hanging from it. "It's a turnip!" cried Eddie. "It's a turnip!"

"No, it isn't a turnip," said Anna Patricia. "It's a radish. That's the way radishes look when they are babies."

"Radishes are red," said Eddie.

"Eddie," said Anna Patricia, "don't you know there are white radishes?"

"Well, I don't care whether it is a radish or

a turnip," said Boodles. "What I want to know is what I have growing in my garden. Those little plants look just like my carrots."

"Let's go see!" said Anna Patricia. The three children ran to get their bicycles. In a few moments they were on their way to Boodles' house.

Hopping off their bicycles, they ran to look at Boodles' garden. "Here they are!" said Boodles. "And there is the picture of the carrot. Carrots should be coming up right where that picture is."

"Oh, Boodles!" said Anna Patricia. "I don't think that's a picture of a carrot. I think that's a banana!"

"A banana!" exclaimed Eddie. "There weren't any banana seeds, Annie Pat! Anyway, bananas grow on trees."

"I know bananas grow on trees," said Anna Patricia. "I just said, the picture is a picture of a banana."

"It's a carrot," said Boodles.

"Well, what's coming up looks just like my turnips," said Eddie.

"You mean your radishes," said Anna Patricia.

"My turnips!" said Eddie. "Pull one up and you'll see. They're turnips." Boodles squatted down and pulled up one of the plants. The children looked at it. "It's a turnip!" exclaimed Eddie.

"It's a radish!" cried Anna Patricia.

"Well, it isn't a carrot," moaned Boodles, "and I don't like turnips."

"Do you like radishes?" asked Anna Patricia.

"Yes, I like radishes," said Boodles.

"Well, what are you worrying about then," said Anna Patricia, "if you like radishes?"

"Because I don't think they are radishes," said Boodles. "I think they are turnips. You and Eddie sold those seeds to me and you cheated me, that's what you did!"

"We did not!" cried Anna Patricia. "It isn't Eddie's and my fault if somebody didn't know how to draw a carrot."

"Well, even if he had known how to draw a carrot, there would have been turnip seeds inside the envelope," said Boodles.

"Radishes," said Anna Patricia.

"Don't try to mix me up!" Boodles cried.

"You sold me the wrong seeds, and it's your fault."

"Say!" cried Anna Patricia. "I wonder what is coming up in my garden. Maybe the pictures are wrong in my garden."

"Let's go see!" said Eddie.

Off went the three children again, on their bicycles. As soon as they reached Anna Patricia's, they ran to the garden. Eddie and Boodles looked at all of the envelopes sticking out of the ground. Anna Patricia had planted string beans, radishes, onions, lettuce, carrots, parsley, cucumbers, cantaloupes, and peas. She also had five tomato plants. "Now we'll see if these little things that are coming up are carrots," said Boodles.

"Of course they are carrots!" said Anna Patricia. "I drew that picture of a carrot myself on that envelope and I draw very well. I got an A in drawing."

Boodles stooped down and pulled up some pale green leaves. Once again the children put their heads together. They looked carefully. There was no yellow root and there was no tiny pink root. "What do you know!" cried Boodles. "It's an onion!"

"But I didn't plant onion seeds," said Anna Patricia. "I put in tiny onions, and now you've pulled one up!"

"Where did you get the onions?" asked Eddie.

"My father bought them for me," said Anna Patricia. "They're called sets. I made the picture of the onion myself."

"Well, what is planted over there where the onion picture is?" asked Eddie.

"I don't know," said Anna Patricia. "I thought they were onions."

"We'll have to pull one up to see," said Eddie. "This is like playing grab bag. You never know what you're going to get."

This time Anna Patricia pulled while the boys watched. Up came a little carrot. "It's a carrot!" Anna Patricia shouted. "I guess I got the pictures mixed."

"You sure are mixed up!" said Eddie. "That isn't a carrot, it's a radish!"

"Silly!" said Anna Patricia, holding the carrot up. "Anybody can see that's a carrot!"

"Radish!" said Eddie, and they all laughed.

Now Boodles began to think about his turnips. "What I want to know," he said, "is what I'm going to do with all those turnips that are coming up in my garden, when I don't like turnips. It's all your fault! You, Anna Patricia Wallace, and you, Eddie Wilson, sold those seeds to me and they were wrong."

"The seeds were not wrong," said Anna Patricia. "The seeds were all right."

"Sure, the seeds were all right," said Eddie. "They came up, didn't they?"

Boodles still looked angry.

"Yes," said Anna Patricia, "if they hadn't been all right, they wouldn't have come up. The picture was wrong."

"That's right!" Eddie agreed. "The picture was wrong. Somebody was dopey and drew the wrong picture."

"I'll tell you what, Boodles," said Anna Patricia. "I'll draw you a nice picture of a turnip, and you can pull out that picture of a banana and put in my picture of a turnip."

"But I'll still have turnips in my garden," said Boodles. "It isn't a picture gallery! It's a garden! And I don't like turnips. How many times do I have to tell you? I don't like turnips!"

"Well, you can sell them and make some money," said Anna Patricia. "Farmers don't eat everything they grow."

"That's right," said Eddie. "You can make a lot of money selling those turnips."

"Where?" asked Boodles. "Where can I sell them? Just tell me."

This question made Eddie's face light up. "Boodles!" he cried. "I've got a swell idea! A real swell idea!" Boodles and Anna Patricia looked at Eddie. "Let's have a vegetable stand, out in front of your house," said Eddie.

The black cloud on Boodles' face cleared. "You mean after school closes?" he said. "When the vegetables are ready to pick?"

"That's right!" said Eddie. "We'll be partners! I'll bring some of my vegetables over to sell."

"Oh, can I bring some too?" asked Anna Patricia. "It will be much nicer than having a lemonade stand."

"Oh, boy!" cried Boodles. "Eddie! You're terrific! That's a swell idea! Maybe people will come from all around to buy my turnips."

As the two boys mounted their bicycles, Anna Patricia said, "I just wonder who made that picture of that carrot that looks like a banana and came up turnips. Whoever it was is awful bad at drawing."

Eddie did some thinking as he wheeled along behind Boodles. When the boys reached Boodles' house, Eddie stopped his bike and said, "Say, Boodles. Don't say anything to Annie Pat, but maybe those things coming up in our gardens are radishes."

"Radishes or turnips," said Boodles, "it doesn't make any difference now. We can sell 'em."

"Sure!" said Eddie. "We can sell 'em!"

Chapter Four

SIDNEY GETS A CROW

IT WAS a warm day late in May when Sidney called through the bushes to Eddie, "Come on over and see what I've got!"

Eddie ran between the bushes. "What have you got?" he said.

"A baby crow," said Sidney.

"Where did you get it?" Eddie asked.

"My uncle was cutting some dead limbs out of his trees," said Sidney, "and when they took one of the limbs down they found a nest with a baby crow in it. He brought it to me, and I'm going to raise it."

"Where have you got it?" asked Eddie.

"Daddy fixed a box with screening over the top and on one side," said Sidney. "Come see it!"

Sidney led Eddie to the back of the house. The box was on a bench not far from the back door. Eddie looked into the box. "It's cute!" he said. "What do you feed it? Birdseed?"

"No, it doesn't like birdseed," said Sidney. "I feed it dog food."

"Dog food!" cried Eddie. "You're kidding!"

"No, I'm not," said Sidney. "He loves it. I don't give him very much. He takes it right off my finger."

"That's some bird!" said Eddie. "I guess it will bark like a dog."

Sidney laughed. "I've named him Big Boy," she said.

"What if he is a girl and lays eggs?" said Eddie.

"Well, then, I'll have to call him Big Girl," said Sidney, "but I think he's a boy. He's very strong, and I think he's going to have a terrible temper."

"Then he's a girl, for sure!" said Eddie, laughing.

During the next weeks the crow grew bigger and ate more and more dog food. Eddie's rabbits grew bigger and ate more and more vegetables. Eddie kept the rabbits in a hutch now.

One Saturday morning, when Eddie was weeding his garden, Sidney came over to talk to him. "Hello, Sid," said Eddie. "This weeding business is hard work, isn't it?"

"Yes, it is," Sidney replied. "Sometimes I forget and then it's awful. It's hard to tell which are the vegetables and which are the weeds."

"How's Big Boy?" Eddie asked. "Has he barked yet?"

Sidney laughed and said, "I let him go."

"Let him go!" cried Eddie, standing up and looking at Sidney. "Don't you like him anymore?"

"Oh, sure I like him," replied Sidney. "He's big and strong now, and I didn't think it was right to keep him in a cage, so I let him go."

"Where will he find dog food? He won't find any up in the trees," said Eddie.

"Oh, he comes to get his dog food," said Sidney. "Don't you hear him in the mornings? He wakes me up and my father and mother, too. He screams for his breakfast so hard he wakes up all the other crows in the neighborhood."

"I guess that's what my mother has been hearing," said Eddie. "She said there were an awful lot of crows around."

"Oh, Big Boy makes the most awful racket!" said Sidney. "I have to get up and go out in my pajamas with a dish of dog food for him."

"Where do you put the dish of dog food?" Eddie asked.

"Oh, I don't put it down," said Sidney. "Big Boy won't eat it out of the dish. He wants to be fed by hand."

"The lazy loafer," said Eddie.

"Yes," said Sidney. "I have to stand there in my pajamas and feed him. When I get through, I go back to bed and go to sleep again."

"What does Big Boy do then?" Eddie asked.

"Oh, he stops yelling and flies off," said Sidney.

"What a bird!" said Eddie.

"I hope I'm not going to have to go out every morning and feed Big Boy forever," said Sidney.

"Maybe if you stopped giving him dog food, he would learn to eat other things," said Eddie.

"I wish he would find some other food he liked," Sidney said with a sigh.

Suddenly Big Boy flew down to the ground. He began pecking in Eddie's garden. "Oh, there's Big Boy now!" said Sidney.

"I see him," said Eddie, "and I see what he's doing. He needn't think he can eat out of my garden! He'd better go on eating dog food." Eddie shouted at the crow, "Shoo! Get out!"

The crow flew up in the air and came down on Eddie's shoulder. "Oh, look!" Sidney cried. "Big Boy's on your shoulder!"

Eddie had never had a bird on his shoulder before, and he wasn't sure that he liked having Big Boy on his shoulder now. Big Boy was a very big bird, and he had a long, sharp beak. Eddie was afraid the crow would peck him on the ear. Instead, Big Boy leaned over and pulled Eddie's favorite pencil right out of

his pocket. In a flash he was off with it. He flew to the roof of the Wilsons' house.

"That crow took my pencil!" cried Eddie, running toward the house and looking up at Big Boy. "It's my favorite pencil!"

"Big Boy! You come down here!" Sidney shouted up at the bird. "You bring that pencil back!"

"He'd better bring it back!" said Eddie.

"He almost took my mother's wristwatch," said Sidney, "when she put it on the porch table. Big Boy was just going to pick it up when Mommy grabbed it."

Big Boy flew back to the garden with Eddie's pencil in his mouth. "Now I'll get it," said Eddie, running back to his garden. Big Boy was playing with the pencil. Eddie couldn't get near him without stepping on his vegetables. "He's a fresh bird!" said Eddie. He picked up his rake and tried to reach the pencil, but the crow was quicker than Eddie. Up went Big Boy, back to the roof.

While the children stood looking up, Big Boy began to walk along the gutter that edged the roof. He carried the pencil in his mouth, like a tightrope walker balancing himself with a pole. When he reached the end of the gutter, he suddenly dropped the pencil. The drainpipe was right there, and the pencil came down the spout. When it popped out at the bottom, Eddie picked it up. Then he shouted up to the bird. "You old smarty! You're just too fresh!"

The crow said, "Caw!" and flew up to the chimney.

"That crow has the loudest caw I ever heard," said Eddie. "It must be from eating all that dog food." Now the crow was walking around the edge of the chimney. "If that crow doesn't watch out—" said Eddie, but before he could say what he was thinking, Big Boy suddenly disappeared.

Sidney cried out, "Oh, there goes Big Boy! He's fallen down the chimney!"

The children rushed into the house and into the living room. They ran to the fireplace and looked on the floor in front of the fireplace. Big Boy was not there. They looked inside among the logs, but the crow was nowhere in sight. "He must be stuck in the chimney!" Sidney cried.

Eddie got into the fireplace with the logs.

He looked up the chimney. "I don't see him," he said.

"He must be there somewhere," said Sidney. "I know he fell down, so he must be there."

"He's probably hiding someplace in this room," said Eddie, pulling himself out of the fireplace. The children began to search the room. They looked on the mantel, but the crow wasn't there. They looked on the windowsills and shook the curtains. They looked behind the chairs and under the sofa. Big Boy was nowhere to be seen.

Suddenly the children heard a rustle in the chimney. They stood still and listened. "He's in the chimney," Sidney whispered. "I hear him." Eddie and Sidney ran back to the fireplace. They were both looking up the chimney when the twins came into the room.

"Who are you looking for? Santa Claus?" asked Joe. "You're going to have a mighty long wait."

"Maybe they're waiting for the wolf who came down the chimney to eat up the three little pigs," said Frank.

"Oh, Frankie!" cried Eddie, pulling his

head out of the chimney. "Sid's crow, Big Boy, fell down the chimney, but he's stuck somewhere."

"Maybe he's on the damper," said Joe. "Let me look!" Eddie moved over and Joe crawled into the fireplace. He looked up the chimney. "That's where he is," he said. "I can hear him. He's up there on the damper."

"Is the damper shut tight?" asked Frank.

"No, it's partly open," Joe replied.

"Isn't there room enough for him to come down?" asked Frank.

"I guess he's afraid," said Joe. "I can see his big mouth. It's wide open."

"Can't you reach up and get him?" Sidney asked.

"My arm isn't long enough," said Joe.

"Open the damper wider," said Frank, "then he'll fall down."

"I might hurt him," said Joe. "He's sitting on it."

"Sid!" said Eddie. "Maybe if you get some dog food, he'll come down to get it."

"Well, I'll go get some," said Sidney. "We can try."

Joe got out of the fireplace and Eddie went

back in. He watched Big Boy until Sidney returned with some dog food on a small dish. "Here it is," she said.

"I'll put the dish on the top of the logs," said Eddie. "Then when he sees it, maybe he'll come down for it."

"I don't think he will," said Sidney. "You know what I told you. He wants to be fed by hand."

The four children sat down beside the fireplace and watched for Big Boy to come down. They sat and waited a long time. Big Boy just rustled around. Every once in a while he gave a faint caw. Finally Sidney said, "He won't come down."

"He's spoiled!" said Eddie.

"Maybe if you held it up the chimney, he would come down," said Frank.

Sidney moved into the fireplace and picked up the dish. She looked up the chimney, and said, "Come on, Big Boy. Come get some nice dinner." Big Boy just looked down at Sidney and chattered. "Nice doggie food," said Sidney in a coaxing voice.

"Caw!" said Big Boy.

"Hold some up in your fingers," said Eddie.

Sidney picked up a bit of the food and held it up the chimney. "Yum, yum," she said. "Doggie food." Big Boy looked down and stayed right on his perch. "I guess he isn't hungry," said Sidney, as she sat back on the floor with the dish in her hand. "Crazy old crow!" she said.

Just then the children heard a car come into the driveway. "Here comes Mum," said Eddie. "She's been to market."

In a few moments Mrs. Wilson came into the room. "What are you doing?" she asked. "What's Joe doing with his head up the chimney?"

"Sid's crow fell down the chimney," said Eddie, "but he won't come all the way down."

"He's sitting on the damper," said Sidney.

Joe pulled his head out, and said, "The damper is open enough for him to come down. He just won't come. He's sitting there with his big mouth open."

"Let me look, Joe," said his mother. Now it was Mrs. Wilson's turn to put her head up the chimney. When she looked up she saw Big Boy perched on the damper. Without waiting another minute, Mrs. Wilson reached up and took hold of the crow. Big Boy squawked and cawed and scolded, but he didn't frighten Mrs. Wilson. She just pulled him down and carried him to the front door. There she let him go. "That is that!" she said.

"Oh, Mrs. Wilson! You're brave!" said Sidney. "Thank you. Did he fly away?"

"Yes," said Mrs. Wilson, "he flew away."

"Sid," said Eddie, as Sidney was about to leave, "keep right on feeding that bird dog food, because I don't want him pecking in my garden."

As the days went by Big Boy came more and more to Eddie's garden. Other crows came too. Eddie decided that Big Boy brought them with him. One day Eddie said to Sidney, "Look here, Sid! Are you still feeding that crow dog food?"

"Well, not as much as I used to," Sidney replied.

"I knew it!" said Eddie. "He's eating out of my garden, and he's brought a lot of his friends to eat in my garden, but I'll fix 'em. I'm going to make a scarecrow."

"I don't see them eating in my garden,"

said Sidney. "But I see rabbits eating in my garden. And you know who has rabbits!"

"Not my rabbits!" said Eddie. "My rabbits are pets. They're not even full grown, and you know I have them in a hutch. I put vegetables out for them and little pellets. They wouldn't think of eating your vegetables, even if they could come into your garden."

"Well, rabbits come into my garden and eat my vegetables, and I'm going to make a scare-rabbit. That's what I'm going to make! A scarerabbit!"

Chapter Five

EDDIE GOES TO A BAZAAR

EDDIE BEGAN at once to think of making his scarecrow. He knew exactly how a scarecrow should look, for he had seen many out in the country. First he had to gather together some old clothes. He asked his mother if there were any of his father's clothes that he could use.

"I cleared out the closets last week," his mother replied. "I gave all the old clothes away for the rummage sale at the church bazaar. I don't think I missed anything."

"Oh, Mum," said Eddie, "that's awful! What am I going to use to make a scarecrow?"

"I really don't know," said his mother.

"Maybe I can get something from Annie Pat's mother," said Eddie.

Later in the day Eddie went over to Anna Patricia's. Her mother, Mrs. Wallace, opened the door. "Hello, Eddie," she said. "Anna Patricia isn't home. She'll be sorry she missed you."

"Well, I didn't really come to see Annie Pat," said Eddie. "I came to ask if you have any old clothes I could use to make a scarecrow."

"I'm sorry, Eddie," said Mrs. Wallace, "but I gave all of our old clothing to the church bazaar."

"Well, O.K.," said Eddie, "thanks anyway."

Eddie stopped at Sidney's and received the same answer from Sidney's mother. "What do you want old clothes for?" asked Sidney.

"I want them to make a scarecrow," said Eddie, "to keep that old crow of yours and all his friends out of my garden. That's what I want the clothes for!"

"Oh," said Sidney. "Well, don't forget I am going to make a scarerabbit to keep the rabbits out of my garden."

"I never heard of a scarerabbit," said Eddie. "How are you going to make it?"

"Oh, I have loads of ideas," said Sidney.

"A scarerabbit!" snorted Eddie. "Who ever heard of a scarerabbit?"

"You're going to hear about it," said Sidney, "and you're going to see it. It's going to scare all the rabbits right out of their skins." Sidney really had no idea how to make a scarerabbit, but she wasn't going to let on to Eddie that she didn't know.

When Eddie reached home, he said to his mother, "I missed getting something for my scarecrow everywhere! Everybody gave their old clothes to the church bazaar. What am I going to do?"

"I guess you will have to buy something at the bazaar," said his mother.

"I don't want to buy old clothes at the bazaar," said Eddie. "I want to spend my money on something else. I might see some valuable property that I would like to buy."

"Oh, Eddie!" his mother exclaimed. "Please don't bring home any more junk!"

"I don't bring home junk, Mum," said Eddie. "It's valuable property."

"It may be valuable property to you, Eddie," said his mother, "but it is junk to me."

The bazaar was to open on Saturday morning at ten o'clock, but Eddie didn't get up when his mother called him. He turned over and went to sleep again. When he finally woke up, he saw that he was going to be late for the opening of the bazaar. "Hey, Mum!" he cried, when he ran into the kitchen. "You didn't call me! I'm late for the bazaar!"

"I did call you, Eddie," said his mother. "You went to sleep again."

"Oh, Mum! I'll miss some valuable property! I just know I will."

"Now don't bring home a lot of junk," said she.

"It will all be gone," said Eddie. "There won't be anything to bring home."

"Well, buy a nice cake for me," said his mother. "Here is some money, and don't lose it."

"I won't lose it," said Eddie, putting the money in his pocket. "I've got a dollar of my own, but I guess I won't spend it. Everything good will be gone."

As soon as Eddie finished his breakfast, he

started for the door. "It's raining," said his mother. "Better wear your slicker."

"Oh, I'll run," said Eddie. "I won't know what to do with my slicker when I take it off."

"Run fast!" said his mother.

Eddie ran. He didn't have to run very far. The church was only two blocks away. When he opened the door, Eddie found a crowd of people inside. They were mostly mothers and children, but there were a few men. Eddie pushed his way through the crowd. Near the door was the table where the cakes were being sold. Eddie saw some beautiful cakes: chocolate cakes, white cakes, orange cakes, coconut cakes, and a beautiful cake with strawberry icing. Eddie was too anxious to find the white elephant table to stop and select a cake. He decided to come back for a cake later.

Eddie pushed on to the white elephant table, his favorite spot at any bazaar. He was always surprised to see what nice things some people gave away for a bazaar. I was stupid to sleep so late, thought Eddie. I hope I didn't miss anything good.

Eddie soon found the table marked *White Elephants.* He worked his way through the crowd around the table until he could see everything on the table. Eddie looked it all over very carefully. He didn't see anything that looked very exciting to him. He guessed that all the good things were gone.

Eddie was disappointed, but just as he was turning away, he saw something behind the counter. A large saleswoman had hidden it from his view. Eddie's eyes popped. This was the real thing! This was valuable property! This was luck! Eddie had never seen anything as good as this at any bazaar. A big leopard's head, with shining eyes and a big open red mouth, gaped at Eddie. A long tongue hung out of the leopard's mouth. The head was resting on the top of a big box, and the paws hung down the sides. Eddie pointed, and said to the woman behind the counter, "What's that, please?"

The woman looked and said, "Oh, that's a leopard rug. Fierce, isn't it?"

"How much is it?" Eddie asked.

"I'll have to find out," the woman replied, "but I don't think your mother would want it because the moths have been in it."

"Oh, my mother wouldn't mind a little thing

like moths," said Eddie. "My mother's very fond of all kinds of animals."

"Well, I don't think that your mother would feel that moths were animals," said the woman.

"How much is it?" asked Eddie.

"I'll have to find out," said the woman again. "Just a minute while I wait on this customer." The woman turned from Eddie to a boy who had asked the price of an old wooden bowl. The boy was a long time in making up his mind. Eddie waited. He stood on one foot and then the other. Once he tried to interrupt, but the woman said, "Just a minute, son. I'll find out about the leopard in just a minute." Eddie waited. He didn't know a minute could be so long.

Suddenly a man walked behind the counter. Eddie saw him pick up the leopard. Then, to Eddie's horror, he saw the man walk away with the valuable property. "Hey, lady!" Eddie cried out. "Somebody is stealing the leopard!"

"Be quiet, boy!" said another saleswoman, who had just come behind the counter. "What is the matter with you?"

"That man!" cried Eddie. "He stole my leopard!"

"What do you mean, *your* leopard?" said the woman. "I sold that rug as soon as the bazaar opened. The man left it here while he did some other shopping."

Eddie was so mad he pounded the table with his fist, and said, "That was my leopard! I wanted that leopard!"

"Stop that," said the woman, "and run along. There is enough noise around here. Run along."

Eddie ran along. He ran all around the bazaar looking for the man with the leopard rug. Finally he spotted him, just as he was about to go out the door. Eddie ran to him, crying, "Mister! Oh, mister!"

The man stopped and looked down at Eddie. "What's your trouble?" he asked.

"Mister," said Eddie, "I guess you don't know that you're carrying something very dangerous!"

"Dangerous?" said the man. "What do you mean? It doesn't look dangerous to me."

"Oh, yes, it is!" said Eddie. "That leopard is full of moths! It's crawling with moths,

and your house will be full of moths. Don't you think you'd better take it back? They'll give you your money back. They're very nice about that."

"Sorry, sonny," said the man. "It doesn't belong to me. I'm just delivering it for a friend, moths and everything."

The man walked away and Eddie saw the leopard disappear into the back of a station wagon. The man locked the doors and walked back toward the bazaar.

Eddie turned away sadly. He didn't care if he never saw that man again. There was no use going back to the white elephant table. There was no valuable property there. He wandered over to the booth where used clothing was being sold. Perhaps he could find something he could use to make his scarecrow.

The best of the secondhand clothes were hanging on racks. There were a great many people looking at the clothes, taking them off the racks and putting them back again. There was a rack marked $5.00, another marked $3.00, and another marked $1.00. Eddie felt that these clothes were all too expensive. He wasn't going to spend his good money and perhaps buy back something that his mother had given to the bazaar.

Eddie pushed through the crowd to a nearby table. On the table was a pile of clothes marked 50¢. Another pile was marked 25¢. Now Eddie had reached the price he was willing to pay—25¢.

Right on top of the 25¢ pile there was a man's hat, and underneath the hat there was a man's raincoat. Eddie picked up the hat. He decided that it would be a fine hat for the scarecrow. Then he picked up the raincoat. It took him only a moment to decide that a raincoat would be fine, too. It would cover a lot of the scarecrow, and it would flap in the wind. It was just the thing to scare the crows! Eddie carried the hat and the raincoat to a woman who was selling the clothes. Eddie heard her say to someone, "Oh, dear! This is awful! Everybody pushing and shoving. I hardly know what I'm doing!"

"I want to buy this hat and this raincoat," said Eddie, holding out two quarters.

"Oh, dear," said the woman. "Where did you get them from?"

"Right off that pile on the table," said Eddie. "The pile marked 25¢."

"All right," said the woman, taking the money from Eddie. "I'm glad somebody can make up his mind. Most of these people can't make up their minds."

Eddie walked away with the hat and the raincoat. Now he would go to the cake table and buy the cake for his mother. He had just selected a big, gooey chocolate cake, when a man rushed up to him and said, "Say, sonny! You've got my hat and raincoat."

Eddie looked up at the man. He was the same man who had carried the leopard out. "Oh, no, sir!" said Eddie. "I just bought this hat and raincoat right over there." Eddie pointed to the clothing section. "You're the man who got the leopard. You're not going to get my hat and raincoat."

"But it's my hat and raincoat!" said the man.

"Well, it was my leopard," said Eddie, "but you didn't let me have it. Now you want to take my hat and raincoat!"

"Look, sonny," said the man, "this is my hat and my raincoat. I wore this hat and this raincoat in here. It's raining outside. I had them on when I came in. I just happened to lay them down on that table over there while I looked for something. They were not for sale. This is my best hat and my new raincoat."

"Oh," said Eddie. "I'm sorry!"

"How much did you pay for these?" the man asked.

"Fifty cents," Eddie replied.

"Well, here's your fifty cents," said the man, handing Eddie two quarters. Eddie handed over the hat and the raincoat. Again Eddie said, "I'm sorry." Then he said, "You didn't say you were sorry about the leopard. You didn't let me pay you for the leopard. Now I haven't got the leopard and I haven't got my scarecrow."

"What do you mean, scarecrow?" asked the man.

"I bought that hat and that raincoat to make a scarecrow," said Eddie.

"My best hat and new raincoat! To make a scarecrow!" exclaimed the man. "Say, sonny, you can have my old hat and my beat-up raincoat to make a scarecrow. You can have them for nothing."

"I can?" said Eddie. "Oh, that's great! And can I have the leopard too?"

"I told you before," said the man, "the leopard doesn't belong to me. The person who owns the leopard has gone to a birthday party."

"Well, whoever it belongs to, they won't like it," said Eddie, "because it's full of moths."

"Look, son," said the man. "You wait here and I'll go home and get my old felt hat and raincoat for you. Will that make you feel better?"

"Yes, sir! I'll feel a lot better," Eddie replied. "I'll wait right by the door, but I sure am sorry about the leopard."

"I'm sorry, too," said the man, "but the person who bought that leopard is crazy about it. Said it was just the thing! I don't know what it's for, but it's just the thing."

"I'll wait for you," said Eddie, "by the door."

The man hurried off and Eddie turned back to the cake table. He paid for the chocolate cake and the saleswoman put it in a box. "Carry it carefully," she said.

"You bet!" said Eddie, as he took the box. Eddie went to the entrance and waited for his new friend to come back with the hat and coat for the scarecrow. It was pouring rain now, and Eddie was sorry he had not worn his slicker.

Right inside the doorway there was a balloon man. It was a very bad day for a balloon man. His big bunch of balloons almost filled the doorway. Eddie looked up at them. They were the kind he liked, big and shiny, and filled with gas that made them tug at the strings. They had faces painted on them. Eddie decided that he couldn't go home without a balloon, so he spent two dimes for a big pink one with a very funny face.

It wasn't long before the man drove up with the old hat and raincoat he had promised to bring back. "Here you are, sonny," he said. "Now make a good scarecrow!"

"Thanks!" said Eddie, as he took the hat and coat from the man. "Thanks a lot!"

The man drove off and Eddie stood in the doorway. He looked at the raindrops bouncing in the street. He knew that he could not run. He would have to walk slowly with the chocolate cake. By the time he reached home the box would be wet right through. That would not be good for the cake. Eddie thought about this. Suddenly he had an idea. Here he was, standing with a raincoat right over his arm and a hat in his hand. Eddie put the cake box down, out of the rain, but he had to hold onto the balloon. First he put his right arm into the raincoat. Then he changed the balloon to the other hand and put his left arm in. The sleeves were so long he thought his hands would never appear. They finally did, but he had a hard time rolling the sleeves up with the balloon in his hand. The coat hung down to the ground, where it fell like a big puddle around his feet. Eddie put the old hat on his head and picked up the cake box. He tucked the box and the balloon under the raincoat. Now he was ready to walk out into the rain.

Anyone watching from a window would have wondered what was walking up the street. It looked like a dwarf in a hat that came almost down to its nose and a long coat that dragged along the wet pavement. It looked very fat and dumpy. No one would have guessed that it was Eddie Wilson, walking home with a chocolate cake and a balloon.

When Eddie woke up on Sunday morning, the sun was shining. He looked out of his bedroom window. Tomorrow was Memorial Day, and he had invited Boodles over to help him make the scarecrow. Then he would be able to look down and see his scarecrow in his garden.

Eddie could see Sidney's garden from his window, too. He looked over into it. Something was sitting in Sid's garden that had not been there before! Eddie looked in amazement. The bright sun was shining on it, and two big eyes were shining right back at Eddie. A large red mouth was open wide, and a red tongue hung out.

Eddie lost no time. He ran over to Sidney's and knocked on the door. "Sid!" he called. "Sid!"

Sidney opened the door, and said, "What's the matter with you, Eddie?"

"That thing in your garden!" Eddie said.

"Oh," said Sidney, "you mean my scare-rabbit! Isn't it super?"

"Who was that man?" said Eddie, because he couldn't think of anything else to say.

"Oh, he's a friend of Daddy's," said Sidney. "I had to leave the bazaar early, because I was going to a birthday party. It was nice of him to bring it home for me." Eddie was still speechless. "Come look at it," said Sidney.

Eddie followed Sidney to her garden. "What's it stuffed with?" Eddie asked.

"There's a little barrel under it," said Sidney.

Eddie looked at the scarerabbit. All he could think to say was, "It's got moths!"

Chapter Six

TROUBLE IN THE GARDENS

ON MONDAY morning, when Boodles arrived, he said to Eddie, "What are you going to use to make the scarecrow?"

"I've got an old pole," said Eddie, "that I can stick into the ground. I cut a piece off and nailed it near the end of the pole to make the shoulders."

"What about the legs and arms?" Boodles asked.

"Oh, the coat sleeves will be the arms, and I don't think he needs legs," said Eddie. "They wouldn't show much, anyway, because the coat is very long."

"What will you use for his head?" asked Boodles.

"Oh, I have a good idea for the head," said Eddie. "I'm going to fasten a balloon on the top of the pole. I bought the balloon at the bazaar."

"A balloon!" said Boodles. "That's a crazy thing to use for a head. What's he going to have for a face? He has to have a face."

"The face is painted on it," Eddie replied.

"Well, he's going to be a funny kind of scarecrow," said Boodles. "No arms and no legs! I'm glad he's going to have a head. Don't you think we should make him some arms and legs?"

"I can't find anything to make them with," said Eddie, "and I'm in a hurry. Sidney already has her scarerabbit in her garden."

"A scarerabbit!" said Boodles. "I never saw a scarerabbit! I want to see it."

"Well, I don't know whether it's a good scarerabbit," said Eddie, "but it sure is valuable property."

"Let's go see it," said Boodles.

Eddie took Boodles to see Sidney's scare-rabbit. When they reached Sidney's garden, Eddie said, "There it is."

Boodles looked at the scarerabbit, and said, "Boy, that's swell! Where did she get it?"

"She got it at the bazaar," Eddie replied. "If she hadn't been there so early, I would have bought it. It's real valuable property."

"It sure is," said Boodles. "Do you think it will scare the rabbits?"

"It wouldn't scare me, if I were a rabbit," said Eddie.

"Do you think your scarecrow is going to scare the crows?" Boodles asked.

"Sure," said Eddie. "Scarecrows always scare the crows. People have been scaring crows with scarecrows for hundreds of years."

"I guess that's the first scarerabbit that was ever made," said Boodles, pointing at the scarerabbit.

"Yepper!" said Eddie. "It's what they call an experiment."

"Maybe Sid will be famous someday," said Boodles, "'cause she invented the scarerab-bit."

As the boys walked back to Eddie's house,

they stopped to look at Eddie's garden. "Have you had any vegetables out of your garden?" Boodles asked.

"My peas will be ready soon," Eddie replied.

"We've been having spinach out of my garden," said Boodles. "Swell spinach."

Eddie and Boodles went inside to finish the scarecrow. "What are you going to do first?" asked Boodles.

"I guess we'd better put the pole in the ground first," said Eddie.

"Where's the balloon?" asked Boodles.

"It's up in my room," replied Eddie. "I'll get it."

In a moment Eddie came down with the balloon. It was on the end of a long string. Boodles looked at the balloon, and said, "Well, it has a funny face. I guess it will look good when it gets the hat on."

"I'll leave it here until we get the pole stuck in the ground," said Eddie. He let go of the string and the balloon went up to the ceiling. Eddie picked up the pole, and said, "Bood, you bring the hammer and the kitchen step-ladder."

The boys carried the things outdoors and

through the yard to the garden. They selected the spot for the scarecrow, and Boodles opened the little stepladder. Eddie climbed up with the pole and stuck it into the ground. Then he hammered on top of the pole until he felt that it would stand firm. He didn't want the scarecrow to fall over after it was finished.

Boodles watched. "Nobody would ever think that was a scarecrow," he said.

Eddie pointed over to Sidney's garden, and said, "Nobody would ever think that thing in Sidney's garden was a scarerabbit."

"They would if you told 'em," said Boodles.

"Well, nobody is going to stand there and tell the rabbits," said Eddie.

"I'm not sure the crows are going to know that this thing is a scarecrow," said Boodles.

"When it's finished it will scare them," said Eddie. "I want to scare that fresh Big Boy! I want to give him a real fright!"

The boys went back to the house. In a few minutes they returned to the garden. Boodles was carrying the hat and the raincoat, and Eddie was carrying the balloon. It was a very windy day, and the balloon whipped about on the end of the string. "I'll put the head on

first," said Eddie, climbing up on the step-ladder.

"How are you going to fasten it?" Boodles asked.

"I drove a couple of nails in, up near the end of the pole," said Eddie. "I'm going to wrap the string around them, real tight."

Boodles stood and watched Eddie as he fastened the balloon to the top of the pole. The balloon wouldn't stay still. The wind shook it even when the string had been wound as tight as Eddie could wind it. "Is he going to shiver all the time?" asked Boodles. "You can name him Shivery Jack. Shivery Jack, the scarecrow!"

The boys laughed about this. "That's good," said Eddie. "Hand up the hat." Boodles handed the hat to Eddie, and Eddie settled it on the balloon head. The old hat covered half the head, and the face peered out from underneath. "Now give me the coat," Eddie said. Boodles handed Eddie the raincoat, and Eddie hung the coat on the shoulders of the scarecrow. "How does he look, Bood?" Eddie asked.

"O.K., I guess," said Boodles, "but he looks awful thin. Button his coat."

Eddie moved around to the front of the scarecrow and looked at the coat. "Oh," he said, "the buttons are all off." Eddie pulled the edges of the coat together. "Looks good, doesn't it?" he said, standing off and looking at the scarecrow.

"It needs something inside of it," Boodles replied, "something to stuff it out. I think it should have arms and legs. I never saw such a skinny scarecrow!"

"Well, I don't have anything to stuff him with," said Eddie. "I think he looks good."

"His head is good," said Boodles. "You were smart to think of that balloon for the head."

Eddie carried the stepladder back to the kitchen, and the boys went into the living room. They sat down to play a game of checkers. Just as Eddie was about to jump Boodles' king, the boys heard Sidney calling from outside, "Eddie! Oh, Eddie!"

"That's Sid," said Eddie. "Don't let's go out until we finish this game."

"No, don't let's," Boodles agreed.

"Eddie!" Sidney called again. "Yoo hoo! Eddie!"

Eddie got up and went to the window. "What do you want?" he yelled. Sidney waved her hand toward the garden and beckoned. Eddie opened the window. "What is it?" he asked.

"Your scarecrow!" Sidney called out. "Your scarecrow blew away!"

"Blew away!" Eddie echoed.

"Yes!" replied Sidney.

"Come on, Bood!" said Eddie, turning away from the window.

The boys rushed outside and joined Sidney. Then they ran to Eddie's garden. There stood the scarecrow with the hat on its head, but the raincoat had blown off and was nowhere in sight. "Poor old Shivery Jack!" cried Boodles. "He's lost his raincoat!" Just as he said it, a gust of wind whipped against the balloon head. The string snapped, and the head went sailing off. "Oh, now he's lost his head!" Boodles cried out.

"His hat is going with it!" cried Eddie. At that moment another gust of wind buffeted the balloon, and the hat fell off. It fell down into Mrs. Wilson's flower garden.

The three children watched as the scarecrow's head went up, up, up, into the blue sky. The grinning face seemed to be laughing at a big joke. The children watched the balloon until it was out of sight. Then Eddie went to his mother's garden and picked up the hat. The children looked around the yard for the raincoat. They looked around the bushes and under the hedge. They looked all the way out to the lawn in front of the house. There, under a bush, Eddie found the raincoat. He looked at it, and said, "I guess I'll have to get my mother to sew some buttons on this coat."

"Have you got another head?" Boodles asked.

"No, I'll have to buy another one," said Eddie.

"I thought they always made scarecrows out of straw," said Boodles. "I never saw one made out of a balloon before."

"I don't have any straw," said Eddie.

"I think my dad has some straw in the garage," said Boodles. "Something came that

was packed in straw, and I don't think he threw the straw away."

"Do you think your father would let me have some of it?" asked Eddie.

"I'll ask him," said Boodles.

"Thanks," said Eddie. "That's great."

By this time the children had walked back to Eddie's garden. They looked up at the bare wooden frame. On the crossbar that Eddie had made for the scarecrow's shoulders sat three big crows. Right on the very top, where Shivery Jack's head had been, Big Boy was perched. "Caw! Caw! Caw!" croaked the crows. Eddie flung the old hat at the crows. The birds scattered, and, to the amazement of the three children, the hat came right down on the piece of the pole that stuck up above the crossbar. Eddie could hardly believe his eyes.

"Good shot!" cried Boodles.

"Eddie! You're super!" said Sidney.

"Oh, it's easy," said Eddie, although he knew he could never do it again if he tried all day.

"Come see my scarerabbit," said Sidney to

Boodles. "I've got a wonderful scarerabbit."

"I saw it," said Boodles, "but I'd like to see it again."

Sidney led the way through the hedge to her garden. She looked at her garden. Boodles looked at the garden, and Eddie looked at the garden. There was no scarerabbit anywhere. Instead there was just a little wooden barrel, and sitting on top of the barrel was a large rabbit. "Where's my scarerabbit?" cried Sidney, in such a loud voice that the rabbit jumped off the barrel and scampered away.

Just then the children heard a noise. It was a dog growling. Eddie ran toward the sound. It came from the other side of the Stewarts' house. He looked through the hedge. There he saw a dog. The dog had the leopard rug in his mouth. He was shaking it with all of his might. "Here it is!" Eddie called to the other children. "A dog's got it!"

Sidney and Boodles looked through the hedge. "It's a dog fight!" Boodles cried.

When Sidney saw what was happening, she screamed, "Don't let him tear up my scarerabbit!"

"He thinks it's a wild animal!" said Boodles.

Eddie ran through the hedge and caught hold of the leopard's tail. He pulled it. "Don't pull the tail off!" Sidney cried.

The dog growled louder, but it was a growl of delight. This was fine! He had a wild animal that couldn't put up a fight. "You coward!" cried Eddie. "Drop it! Drop it!"

Suddenly the dog was quiet. He stood still with his mouth full of leopard rug. The leopard's head hung out of the side of his mouth. He looked so funny that Boodles laughed. Then Eddie laughed, and even Sidney laughed. The dog looked sheepish. He knew the children were laughing at him. He dropped the leopard and walked away.

Eddie picked up the rug and carried it back to Sidney's garden. He put it over the barrel, and said, "Sid, you'd better put some rocks on it to hold it down."

"Thanks, Eddie, for rescuing my scarerabbit," said Sidney.

"Oh, that's O.K.," said Eddie. "I hope that dog doesn't come back and pick on it anymore, 'cause I don't want that leopard to get any more holes in it."

"What do you mean? It isn't your leopard," said Sidney. "It's my scarerabbit."

"I know it isn't my leopard," said Eddie, "but I wasn't going to let a dog have it. As long as I can't have it, I would rather let you have it than let a dog have it."

"Well, thanks!" said Sidney. "I'm glad I'm better than a dog!"

Eddie and Boodles watched Sidney as she walked away with her nose in the air. "Now what's the matter with her?" asked Eddie.

"Oh, you never can tell about girls," said Boodles. "They get mad over nothing!"

Chapter Seven

HOW DOES HIS GARDEN GROW?

THE SCARECROW that finally watched over Eddie's garden was very different from the balloon scarecrow. Boodles' father helped the boys make it of straw, and Eddie was delighted with the results. He was sure that the scarecrow kept the crows away, and Sidney was certain that her scarerabbit kept the rabbits out of her garden. The children never saw what went on while they were in school or off on their bicycles, but the gardens continued to grow.

By the time school closed for the summer vacation, many of the gardens had vegetables ready to be picked. Everyone was growing peas and carrots, and Mrs. Bolling had been receiving presents of radishes from the children for several weeks.

The day school closed Boodles went over to see Eddie at his house. He found Eddie and Anna Patricia sitting in the kitchen, having milk and cookies. "Hello, Bood," said Eddie. "Have some milk and cookies."

"Thanks," said Boodles.

Eddie poured a glass of milk for Boodles, and Boodles sat down beside Anna Patricia, who passed the plate of cookies to him. Boodles took a swallow of milk, and said, "My father and mother are taking me and my sister to the seashore for our vacation. We're going next week."

"That's swell!" said Eddie.

"I was wondering," said Boodles. "Eddie, could you take care of my garden while we're away?"

"I guess so," said Eddie.

"You won't have to do very much," said Boodles. "Of course, you'll have to water it."

"Sure," said Eddie.

"And pull up the weeds," said Boodles.

"Uh, huh," said Eddie.

"But be careful not to pull up my sunflowers," said Boodles.

"O.K.," said Eddie.

"Keep the dirt nice and crumbly," said Boodles. "You'll find all the tools in the garage."

"Uh, huh," said Eddie.

"Be sure to watch out for bugs," said Boodles. "I don't want any Mexican bean beetles on my beans."

"Mexican jumping bean beetles!" said Anna Patricia. "I never heard of Mexican jumping bean beetles."

"Not Mexican jumping bean beetles," said Boodles. "Mexican beetle beans."

"No," said Anna Patricia, "that isn't what you said the first time. You said Mexican jumping beetles."

"No, I didn't!" Boodles replied. "Annie Pat, you're getting me all mixed up."

"Yes! You keep out of this, Annie Pat,"

said Eddie. "You get everything mixed up. They're Mexican beetle jumpers."

"No, no!" cried Boodles. "They are not jumping beetles. I didn't say anything about jumping. You were the one who said jumping. They're just plain bean beetles."

"If they were plain bean beetles," said Anna Patricia, "they would call them plain bean beetles. They are Mexican bean beetles, so they are not plain."

"O.K., O.K.!" said Boodles.

"Now you have to watch out for cucumber hoppers," said Boodles. "No, I mean cucumber beetles. They're called striped cucumber beetles."

"Oh!" cried Anna Patricia. "Pickle beetles! Do their stripes go round and round, like a sweater, or over and over?" This made the boys laugh.

"Say, Boodles," said Eddie. "I can't remember all those things."

"Oh, it's easy," said Boodles. "Just one other thing about bugs."

"What?" asked Eddie.

"Watch the tomato plants," replied Boodles.

"What for?" Eddie asked.

"Tobacco worms," said Boodles.

"Tobacco worms!" exclaimed Anna Patricia. "Why don't they call them tomato worms?"

"I don't know why they call them tobacco worms," said Boodles. "But I know what they look like. They are long green caterpillars, with white stripes and yellow spots."

"Well, if they are caterpillars, why don't they call them caterpillars?" said Anna Patricia.

"Maybe because caterpillars turn into butterflies," said Eddie, "and maybe these tobacco things don't turn into butterflies."

"Maybe they spit tobacco," said Boodles, "like grasshoppers."

"Maybe they smoke a pipe!" exclaimed Anna Patricia.

"You're simpleminded, Annie Pat," said Boodles, "just simpleminded."

"I am not simpleminded!" replied Anna Patricia. "The caterpillar in *Alice in Wonderland* smoked a pipe. I can show you the picture in my *Alice in Wonderland* book."

"Well, never mind *Alice in Wonderland!*"

aid Boodles. "These bugs I'm talking about are called tobacco worms."

"How do you know about jumping beetles and all these worms and things?" asked Anna Patricia.

"My grandfather lives on a farm," said Boodles, "and he wrote me a letter all about them."

"Well, say, Bood," said Eddie. "Are you raising bugs or vegetables?"

"I like bugs," said Boodles. "I can sit and watch a bug all day."

"Then why don't you let the bugs eat up all the vegetables? When you come home you'll have a lot of bugs to watch, and I won't have to take care of your garden," said Eddie.

"Eddie!" exclaimed Boodles. "You said we were going to have a vegetable stand. How can we have a vegetable stand if you don't take care of my vegetable garden?"

"O.K.," said Eddie. "I'll watch out for the bugs."

"Well, so long," said Boodles. "Thanks a lot."

"So long," said Eddie.

The next weeks were the busiest weeks

Eddie had ever known. He was glad he had a bicycle. He bicycled back and forth from his own garden to Boodles' garden every other day. The weather was very hot, and there was no rain. Eddie had to water his garden, and then he had to water Boodles' garden. The hose at Boodles' house wasn't long enough to reach the garden, so Eddie had to water the garden with a watering can. Sometimes Anna Patricia came over and helped Eddie. Anna Patricia had become very good at weeding.

When Boodles had been away for a week, Eddie received a card from him. He had written on the back of the card, "Having a fine time. Wish you were here. Am having a birthday party on July 7. Sorry you can't come. We go to the post office to get packages. So long! Boodles."

The next day, while Eddie was working in Boodles' garden, Anna Patricia arrived. "Hi, Eddie," she said. "Boodles is going to have a birthday party. I got a postcard."

"I know," said Eddie. "He sent me one, too."

"I don't know why he doesn't have his birthday party after he comes home," said Anna

Patricia. "I think he's real mean, after all the work we've done in his garden!"

"Well, he won't get any birthday present from me," said Eddie.

"Me either," said Anna Patricia. "He put his address on my postcard. He said he was writing it down in case I needed it."

"He sent it to me, too," said Eddie.

"What would we need his address for?" asked Anna Patricia, leaning over to look at Boodles' tomato plants. Suddenly she cried out, "Oh, Eddie! Come look! Here is one of those smoking caterpillars!"

Eddie came running to Anna Patricia. "You mean tobacco worms," said Eddie, looking at the worm. "Say, it's pretty, isn't it? And look at that spike sticking out of its end."

"Here's another one!" said Anna Patricia, pointing to another leaf.

Anna Patricia was very quiet. She was thinking. Then she said, "Eddie, I've got an idea. Let's send these caterpillars to Boodles."

Eddie looked at Anna Patricia, and said, "Annie Pat, sometimes you are real smart."

A grin spread over Anna Patricia's face,

and she said, "I know something even better."

"What?" asked Eddie.

"Let's send them to him for his birthday," she said.

"Hot diggety!" shouted Eddie. "That's super! We'll send 'em to him for his birthday, and he can sit and watch 'em. He said he could sit and watch a bug all day!"

"I wish we could find one of those Mexican hopping beetles," said Anna Patricia.

"You mean Mexican jumping bean beetles," said Eddie. "Let's look. Maybe we can find one."

"Well, first we have to put these worms in a box," said Anna Patricia. "We don't want to lose them."

"We'll have to feed them," said Eddie. "We can't let 'em starve."

"That's right," said Anna Patricia, "we'll fatten them up."

Eddie laughed. "Boodles isn't going to eat these bugs," he said.

"I know he isn't," said Anna Patricia, "but we want them to look good."

"Now you watch them," said Eddie. "Don't

let them get away. I'll look in the garage and see if I can find a box to put them in."

Anna Patricia picked the leaves that the worms were eating and held them in her hand. "Hurry up!" she called.

Eddie hurried to the garage and soon came back with a battered shoe box. "Here, we can put them in this box," he said. He held the box out to Anna Patricia, and she dropped the leaves with the worms into it. "Now pick some leaves so that they will have something to eat," said Eddie.

The children covered the bottom of the box with tomato leaves. "If they eat all those leaves, they'll be as big as sausages!" said Eddie, as he put the lid on the box. "I'll leave the box here in the garage," he added.

"Maybe we can find a Mexican beanel beet now," said Anna Patricia. Eddie roared with laughter. "I mean a Mexican beetle bean!" said Anna Patricia. Eddie laughed harder than ever. "Oh, what are they?" asked Anna Patricia.

"They're Mexican bean beetles!" said Eddie, when he finally stopped laughing.

"Well, I wish we could find one," said Anna Patricia.

"Maybe you will," said Eddie, "but I hope we don't find any more tobacco worms." Eddie didn't want the plants to get full of these pests.

Eddie and Anna Patricia came to Boodles' garden every day. They always looked in the box at the tobacco worms to see if they were all right. A few days before Boodles' birthday, Eddie said, "I guess we won't find a Mexican bean beetle."

"Oh, let's look real hard," said Anna Patricia.

The children looked all through the beans. Finally Eddie cried out, "I think I've found one! Look!" Anna Patricia came to Eddie and stooped down. "See," said Eddie, pointing to a spot on the ground.

Anna Patricia looked at the bug very carefully. It had copper-colored wings, and each wing had eight black spots. "That's pretty," said Anna Patricia, "but I think it's dead."

"Well, a dead one is better than none at all," said Eddie.

"That's right," Anna Patricia agreed. "Let's send it to Boodles."

Eddie went off for the shoe box. When he returned, he said, "Here, put it in."

Anna Patricia picked up the beetle and put it in the box. "Now we have to wrap the box in some pretty paper," she said. "I have some at my house. Let's do it now."

Eddie and Anna Patricia hopped on their bicycles and soon they arrived at Anna Patricia's. "I have a little box that we can put them in," she said. "It will look more like a birthday present."

Eddie took the beetle and the worms out of the shoe box and placed them in the little box. Then he wrapped it in some flowered paper and tied it with some blue ribbon that Anna Patricia gave him. Anna Patricia had bought a birthday card, and both of the children wrote their names on it. They stuck the card under the ribbon bow. Anna Patricia giggled. "Boodles will be surprised when he opens this birthday present," she said.

Eddie laughed. "Well, we're sending him something he said he was crazy about," he said. "I never got a present that I wanted to look at all day, except my bicycle." Eddie wrapped the box in brown paper, and printed Boodles' name and address on the outside.

"Now let's take it to the post office," said Anna Patricia.

"I'll carry it," said Eddie, " 'cause I can carry it easy in my bike bag."

The children soon reached the post office. Eddie handed the parcel to the clerk who was behind the counter. "What's this?" asked the man.

"It's a birthday present," Eddie replied.

"I mean, what's in the package?" said the man.

"Some bugs," said Eddie.

"Bugs!" exclaimed the man. "What kind of bugs?"

"Two tobacco worms," said Eddie. "And—"

Anna Patricia interrupted. "Isn't that a funny name for a worm?" she asked the man.

"Are these some kind of toys?" asked the man.

"Oh, no. They're alive," Eddie answered.

"Alive!" cried the man. "Don't you know it's against the law to send live bugs and worms through the mail? There's a great big fine and you could go to jail."

The children's eyes grew very big. "Oh!" exclaimed Eddie. "I didn't know that."

"We won't get arrested, will we?" asked Anna Patricia, in a very small voice.

"Not this time," said the man, "but don't ever forget it."

"Couldn't we just send the Mexican bean beetle?" asked Eddie. "It's dead."

"No siree!" said the man. "No dead bugs can go through the mail. Take it away!" The man pushed the parcel away.

The children left the post office with their parcel. "What shall we do with it?" Eddie asked Anna Patricia.

"Let's take the birthday card out of it," said Anna Patricia. "We can send that to Boodles." The children sat down on the steps of the post office and unwrapped the package. Anna Patricia removed the birthday card, and said, "Here, Eddie. You write Boodles' address on the envelope."

Eddie took his ball-point pen out of his pocket. He took the card out of its envelope and added a few words under their names.

Anna Patricia looked over Eddie's shoulder. Now the card said, "Happy Birthday to Boodles from Anna Patricia and Eddie and a dead Mexican jumping bean beetle and two smoky worms."

"It's a shame we couldn't send the bugs," said Anna Patricia, "but I'm glad we didn't get arrested."

"And go to jail!" said Eddie. "Would my father have been mad!"

Chapter Eight

THE VEGETABLE STAND

EDDIE HAD begun to wonder whether Boodles would ever come back to take care of his own garden. It seemed like more than three weeks since he had gone away. At last the day came when Boodles telephoned Eddie. "Hi, Eddie!" he said. "I'm home!"

Eddie had never been so glad to hear from anyone. "Hi, Boodles!" he replied. "Boy, am I glad you're home! I thought you would never come back!"

"The garden looks swell," said Boodles. "I guess you have a green thumb, all right. How's your garden?"

"Great!" replied Eddie. "I think I'm growing the biggest watermelon in the whole world. It's enormous! You should see it."

"Maybe it will win a prize," said Boodles.

"That's what I'm hoping for," said Eddie. "A prize watermelon."

"How's the scarecrow?" asked Boodles.

"O.K.," Eddie replied.

"Does he keep the crows away?" Boodles asked.

"Well, he doesn't scare Big Boy," Eddie replied. "He's as fresh and sassy as ever. He sure likes company. If Sidney is away, Big Boy comes right over to us."

"How are your rabbits?" asked Boodles.

"They're fine," replied Eddie. "Wait until you see how big they are! Dad says I ought to specialize in rabbits and watermelons."

"Have you let them go," asked Boodles, "or are they still in the hutch?"

"Oh, they're tame rabbits now," said Eddie. "A dog would get them if I let them go."

"How is Sidney's scarerabbit?" asked Boodles.

Eddie laughed. "It's still sitting in Sid's garden."

"Is it scaring the rabbits?" asked Boodles.

"Sid says it's scaring them to death," Eddie replied, "but every time I look at it, there's a rabbit sitting on the scarerabbit's back."

"How about our vegetable stand?" asked Boodles. "I have to sell those turnips. Remember about those turnips? You and Anna Patricia got me all mixed up with those seeds, remember?"

"I'd like to sell some of my vegetables, too," said Eddie. "We've been eating string beans until they're coming out of the top of my head. Annie Pat has carrots and beets."

"What about Sidney?" Boodles asked. "Does she want to come in on our vegetable stand?"

"Oh, sure," replied Eddie. "Sid won't want to miss that. She's loaded with parsley."

"Well, how about it?" said Boodles. "Can we get our stand set up next week?"

"Sure!" said Eddie. "I'll tell the girls."

"Come over on Monday morning," said Boodles.

"O.K.," said Eddie. "So long."

"So long," Boodles answered. "Thanks for taking care of my garden."

Eddie and Sidney and Anna Patricia agreed to meet at Boodles' house on Monday morning. Eddie got up early and went out to pick his string beans. Even early in the morning he could see that it was going to be a very hot day. Eddie put the beans in a basket as he picked them.

Sidney was already sitting on her back steps, tying bunches of parsley. "How much money do you think we'll make?" she called over the hedge to Eddie.

"I don't know," Eddie replied, "but these are real fresh vegetables. I guess we ought to make a lot."

"I'm tying my bunches of parsley with ribbon," said Sidney. "I have a lot of old Christmas ribbons that came off packages last Christmas." Sidney held up a bunch of parsley tied with red ribbon. "Looks like Christmas, doesn't it?"

"Oh, it looks great!" said Eddie, but he thought to himself, that's just like a girl, tying up parsley with red ribbon. Christmas! It wasn't even August!

"You need something different, to make people in cars stop," said Sidney.

"Yep," said Eddie. "I made a sign. It says *Fresh Vegetables for Sale."*

"Oh, that's good," said Sidney, as she went back to her parsley and Christmas ribbons.

When Eddie had his basket filled with beans, he put the basket in his express wagon. He put a small strawberry box in the wagon, to use as a measure, and a package of paper bags. Then he pulled the wagon around to where Sidney was bunching her parsley. "Don't they look pretty?" said Sidney.

"Sure," said Eddie, "but I feel sort of silly selling parsley all tied up with ribbons. It's the sissiest looking parsley I ever saw."

"Well, you don't have to sell it," said Sidney. "It's my parsley, and I'll sell it."

"I just hope Annie Pat doesn't bring a lot of sissy looking carrots," said Eddie.

"Where's your sign?" asked Sidney, looking at the wagon, as they set out for Boodles' house.

"In the bottom of the wagon," said Eddie.

When Eddie and Sidney arrived at Boodles' house, they found Boodles and Anna Patricia setting up two card tables right beside the en-

FRESH
VEGETABLES
FOR SALE

trance to the driveway, under a big tree. "Hi, Eddie!" Boodles shouted. "Do you think this is a good place for the vegetable stand?"

"Couldn't be better," said Eddie. "This tree will shade the vegetables."

"Look at my bunches of parsley," said Sidney to Anna Patricia.

"Oh, Sidney!" cried Anna Patricia. "Aren't they pretty! They look like Christmas."

"That's what I think," said Sidney.

"Christmas!" cried Boodles, wiping the perspiration from his face.

"Pretty parsley!" cried Eddie. "Let me put my pretty string beans on the table."

"Sure, Santa Claus," said Boodles. "Step right up with your pretty string beans."

"Where are your pretty turnips, Boodles?" asked Eddie.

"They're in the garage with my pretty reindeer," replied Boodles, laughing.

"I hope your pretty reindeer won't eat your pretty turnips," said Eddie, as he placed the basket of beans on the table.

"You boys are so silly," said Sidney.

"Yes," said Anna Patricia. "Just you wait and see. All the cars will stop to buy those bunches of parsley. Sidney, why don't we arrange them on the table, like wreaths?"

"Oh, that's a good idea," said Sidney.

"Wreaths!" cried Eddie.

"Maybe we should build a snowman," said Boodles. "It's such a hot day."

Boodles took Eddie's express wagon to the garage and came back with a carton filled with turnips. Eddie looked at the turnips, and said, "What pretty turnips! Or are they Christmas-tree balls?" Boodles and Eddie laughed so hard over this joke that they had to lean against the table.

"Eddie, you're simple," said Anna Patricia. "Stop shaking the table. You're knocking these wreaths apart."

"Eddie, where's the sign that you made?" said Sidney.

"It's right here," replied Eddie, pulling the sign out of the bottom of the express wagon.

"Well, put it up," said Sidney, "and stop being so silly. Don't you see the cars going by? We have to get customers."

"O.K.," said Eddie, looking around. "Where shall I put it?"

"Tack it on the trunk of the tree," said

Boodles. "I'll get you some tacks." Boodles went into the house, and came back with a hammer and tacks. He held the sign while Eddie fastened it to the trunk of the tree.

Sidney picked up a bunch of parsley and waved it at a passing car, but the car went by. "Here comes another one," said Eddie, putting down his hammer. As the car came near, Eddie pointed to the sign. The car drove by.

Suddenly Sidney heard a familiar sound. "Caw! Caw!"

"Oh, there's Big Boy!" she said. "He's found us." Sidney looked up into the tree. Sure enough, there sat Big Boy on a low limb.

Eddie looked up. "Every time I see that bird, I look for trouble," he said.

"You're just jealous," said Sidney, "because your rabbits don't follow you the way Big Boy follows me."

"Well, my rabbits don't fall down people's chimneys," said Eddie, "and they're not thieves."

"Big Boy is not a thief!" said Sidney. "He's just playful." She held up a bunch of parsley as a car passed.

"Playful!" said Eddie. "If he were a person, he would be in jail." Eddie pointed to the sign as another car went by. "I don't know why no cars will stop," he said.

"Here are all these beautiful vegetables," said Anna Patricia, "and they go right by."

"Yes," said Sidney. "I don't want my parsley to get wilted."

"I don't know what's the matter with these people," said Eddie.

"If they would just stop and see these pretty wreaths of parsley, they would buy our vegetables," said Anna Patricia.

"Maybe the sign isn't big enough," said Boodles.

"Sure it's big enough," said Eddie.

"I think it should say *Stop,"* said Sidney.

"Yes. I think it should say *Stop,"* Anna Patricia agreed.

"There's some red paint on the shelf in the garage," said Boodles. "I'll go get it."

While Boodles ran to the garage, Sidney and Anna Patricia tried to attract the people in the passing cars. Most of the people smiled at the children, but no one stopped. Eddie stood by the tree. He was going through old cards and pieces of paper that he had taken out of his pocket.

When Boodles came back with the can of paint, he had a brush, too. "Come on, Eddie," he said. "Put *Stop* on the sign."

Eddie didn't pay any attention. Instead he was counting out loud while he looked at a little card in his hand. "Eddie!" said Boodles. "Get to work!"

Eddie took the can and the brush. He was saying over and over, "One hundred and twenty-nine, one hundred and twenty-nine, one hundred and twenty-nine."

"One hundred and twenty-nine what?" asked Anna Patricia.

Eddie didn't reply. He dipped the brush into the can of red paint and looked at the sign. The children watched him. They forgot about the cars and gathered around the trunk of the tree. They watched Eddie as he painted red letters under the black letters. As he worked, the children were more and more puzzled, for Eddie was not printing the word *Stop*. Instead, when he had finished, the children read, *Buy Now! Only* 129 *Days Until Christmas!*

"Oh, boy!" Boodles shouted.

"That will make them stop!" Anna Patricia cried.

"Now they will see my wreaths of parsley!" cried Sidney.

"I know something!" Boodles shouted, as he ran back to the garage. In a moment he reappeared. He ran down the driveway to the children, shaking an old string of sleigh bells.

A car, coming down the street, heard the sound of the sleigh bells. It slowed down, and the man and the woman in the car read the sign, *Buy Now! Only* 129 *Days Until Christmas!* They laughed and stopped the car. The woman stepped out, and said, "What nice vegetables, and what pretty parsley!" Sidney made a face at Eddie, and Eddie grinned.

The woman bought some beans and some carrots and a bunch of parsley. Then she looked at Boodles' turnips, and said, "What lovely turnips!"

"They're really Christmas-tree balls," said Boodles, "but some people call them turnips." Everyone laughed.

After the woman had bought some turnips, Eddie counted up the amount the woman owed them for all of the vegetables. It came to sixty-five cents. She handed Boodles a dollar bill. "I'll have to get some change from my mother," said Boodles. "I won't be a minute."

Big Boy was perched on the sleigh bells. He was trying to pick one of the bells off. As he moved around he made the bells jingle. "What a funny crow," said the woman, as she waited for her change.

"He's mine," said Sidney. "He follows me all around."

Boodles came running back with the dollar in one hand and thirty-five cents in the other. "I'm sorry I had to keep you waiting," he said. "Thanks for stopping."

"I hope you have a lot of customers," the woman said, as she got into her car.

"Thanks!" the children called back. Boodles put the dollar bill on the back edge of the table.

Another car stopped. A man stepped out. "I couldn't go past that sign," said the man with a laugh.

"We have very nice string beans," said Eddie. "Just picked this morning."

"I'll take some, and some carrots, too," said the man.

Eddie measured the beans into a bag. "That will be thirty cents, and fifteen for the carrots."

The man handed Eddie forty-five cents. As he turned away, he said, "Well, Merry Christmas!"

The children laughed and called back, "Merry Christmas!"

"Hey, Boodles," Eddie said, as the man drove off, "where do we keep the money?"

"I guess we should have a box," said Boodles. "I'll see if there is one in the garage." Boodles ran off to the garage again. He came back with an empty shoe box. "Here," he said, "put the money in this box." Eddie put the forty-five cents in the box. "Where's the dollar I left here on the table?" asked Boodles.

"I didn't see it," said Eddie.

"I guess you put it in your pocket," said Anna Patricia.

"No, I didn't!" shouted Boodles. "I put it right here on the table. I know I did!" Just to make sure, Boodles felt in all of his pockets, but he did not find the dollar. "That's very funny," he said. "I put that dollar right here on the back of this table."

"Maybe it blew away," said Sidney. The children looked all through the vegetables. They looked under the table. They looked around in the grass.

Every few minutes cars stopped, and they had to stop looking for the dollar and sell vegetables. Between sales, Boodles watched for cars and shook the sleigh bells to attract attention. The other three hunted through the grass for the dollar bill.

By one o'clock the children had sold all their vegetables, but they had not found the lost dollar. Eddie counted the money in the box. There was five dollars and sixty-five cents all together. "If we could find that dollar, we would have six dollars and sixty-five cents. This vegetable business is a good business!" said Eddie.

"How much do we each get?" asked Anna Patricia.

"Well, I ought to get the most," said Eddie, "because beans always cost more than carrots and parsley and turnips."

"Why, Eddie Wilson!" said Anna Patricia.

"We sold all of the packages of seeds for the same price, and you got your seeds for nothing. Don't forget that! All the money should be divided equally."

"All right," said Eddie. "I'll figure out how much we each get. I'll put it down on the edge of this newspaper." Eddie felt in his pocket for his pencil. It wasn't there. He looked around on the table. "Did anybody see my pencil?" he asked.

Each of the children said, "I didn't see it."

"It's my best pencil!" said Eddie. Then he thought for a moment, and said, "It's the same one that your crow stole, Sid. You remember—he took it up to the roof, and I never would have gotten it back if he hadn't dropped it down the rainspout."

Sidney's eyes opened very wide. She looked around, and asked, "Where is Big Boy? I haven't seen him for a long time."

"The last time I saw him he was working on one of those bells," said Boodles.

"Do you know what?" said Eddie.

"Yep," said Boodles. "I know."

"He stole our dollar!" the children shouted in a chorus.

"And he stole my pencil again," said Eddie.

"But where did he take them?" asked Sidney. "That's the mystery!"

"What a bird!" said Eddie. "What a bird!"

Chapter Nine

EDDIE'S GREEN THUMB

THERE WERE only a few days during August when the vegetable stand was put up under the big tree. Most of the vegetables from the children's gardens were just enough for their own families. Eddie was sorry, because he thought it great fun to put up signs that made the cars stop at the stand. One said, *Stop, Vegetables! Look, Vegetables!* Another said, *Farmers Working! Drive Slowly!*

Big Boy still came with Sidney, but the children watched him carefully. Every once in a while, one of the children would say, "I wonder where that dollar is."

Eddie would add, "And my best pencil!"

All during the month Eddie watched his watermelon patch. The big watermelon grew larger and larger. It grew so big that all of Eddie's friends came to see it. "Are you going to sell it on our vegetable stand?" Anna Patricia asked one day, when she and Boodles were looking at Eddie's garden.

"Eddie wouldn't be able to get it onto the table," said Boodles. "He wouldn't be able to lift it."

"It will be even heavier when it's ripe," said Eddie.

"It's a prize watermelon all right," said Boodles.

"You've got a green thumb for sure, Eddie," said Anna Patricia.

"Anybody who can grow a watermelon that big has green fingers, too," said Boodles.

"I have some very big tomatoes," said Anna Patricia. "Real prize tomatoes."

When school opened in September, the children in Eddie's class were delighted to learn that Mrs. Bolling had been promoted. She was their teacher again. It was Mrs. Bolling who had suggested that they have gardens. It was she who had thought of the Green

Thumb project. Now she was anxious to hear about the children's gardens. They all had a great deal to tell.

"You should see my watermelon, Mrs. Bolling," said Eddie. "I only have one, but it's a prize watermelon. And it's almost ready to pick."

"I've got some prize tomatoes," said Anna Patricia.

"I have some swell turnips," said Boodles.

Many of the children told about their gardens. When they had finished, Mrs. Bolling said, "Suppose we have a garden show! We'll see how many green thumbs we have in this class."

"Will there be a prize?" asked Boodles.

"No," said Mrs. Bolling. "It would hardly be fair to choose between a prize ear of corn and a prize watermelon."

"I think everybody who brings something for the show should get an award," said Sidney, "because it's hard work to raise vegetables."

"That's true, Sidney," Mrs. Bolling agreed.

"Yes," said Alex, "and sometimes you don't

get anything but worms and beetles and bugs."

"And rabbits!" said Sidney.

"And crows!" said Eddie.

"That's right," said Anna Patricia, "and smoky worms and jumping bean beetles from Mexico."

"She means Mexican bean beetles and tobacco worms," said Eddie. "She always gets it all mixed up."

"We'll have the Green Thumb Show on Wednesday," said Mrs. Bolling.

"I'll bring my watermelon," said Eddie. "Then at lunchtime you can cut it, Mrs. Bolling, and everyone in the class can have a piece."

"That is very generous, Eddie," said Mrs. Bolling.

On Tuesday Eddie hurried home from school. He was going to pick his watermelon at last! When he reached home, he said to his mother, "Mum! I'm going to pick my watermelon. Can you make room in the refrigerator? I want it to be real cold when I take it to school tomorrow. I'm going to share it with the class."

"I shall have to empty a whole shelf to hold that watermelon," said his mother, laughing. "How are you ever going to get it to school?"

"In my express wagon," said Eddie.

Mrs. Wilson began to empty a shelf in the refrigerator. "This sure is exciting, isn't it, Mum?" said Eddie. "I've been watching that watermelon get bigger and bigger for a long time."

Eddie went out to his garden. His watermelon patch had produced only one watermelon, but what a watermelon it was! Eddie knelt down beside it and thumped it. It sounded the way Eddie thought a ripe watermelon should sound. Everything was right about this watermelon. It was a rich dark green with light green markings. It was perfectly shaped, long and oval. Just looking at it made Eddie's mouth water.

Eddie wiggled the stem and the melon broke free. He rolled it over. He was delighted to see that the underside of the melon was just as perfect as the topside. Eddie picked it up. It was heavy. It was heavier than he had thought it would be. He knew at once that it was too heavy for him to carry

to the kitchen. He would have to put it in his express wagon and pull it to the kitchen door.

The express wagon was standing in the driveway near the garage. Eddie was sure he could carry the watermelon that far. He heaved it up higher into his arms and took a few steps toward the wagon. He stopped and heaved the watermelon again. Now he had a firmer grip on it. It was a bit slippery. He took a few more steps. He hadn't far to go now.

Just as he was about to step onto the driveway, Eddie stumbled on a stone in the grass. He lost his balance and let go of the watermelon. Down it crashed on the hard driveway right beside the express wagon. It broke into many juicy chunks, splashing pink juice all around.

Eddie looked down at the broken watermelon. He could hardly believe that what he saw was true. This could not be his beautiful watermelon, lying in juicy pieces! For a moment he did not know what to do. He just stood there, looking down at his feet. The pieces of watermelon soon became blurred as tears filled Eddie's eyes. He bit his lip, trying not to cry. His prize watermelon! Dropped! And he had dropped it.

Now he was mad. He gave his express wagon a terrible kick. It rattled toward the garage door and bumped against it. Eddie wished he could kick himself. "Clumsy lummox!" he said aloud. "Clumsy lummox!"

Just at that moment Sidney came through the hedge. Eddie choked back his tears. He wasn't going to let Sidney see him cry.

"Eddie!" cried Sidney, when she saw the watermelon mess. "Eddie, what happened?"

"Can't you see?" cried Eddie.

"But what happened?" said Sidney.

"I dropped it," replied Eddie. "I tripped over that stone." Eddie picked up the stone and flung it with all his might.

"Oh, Eddie!" said Sidney. "Is it your nice watermelon that you were going to take to school?"

"Of course!" said Eddie. "Don't be so stupid! What other watermelon did I have?"

"Well, don't be so rude," said Sidney. "I'm being sympathetic. You don't call people stupid when they're being sympathetic."

"I'm sorry, Sid," said Eddie. "I didn't mean it. I'm just mad."

"Well, let's pick up the good parts," said Sidney. "There are a lot of very nice pieces here that don't have any dirt on them." Eddie brought his express wagon back. Then he and Sidney picked up the pieces. "Now, Eddie," said Sidney, "you just take these pieces to school and everybody will be able to see what a big watermelon you grew."

"Do you think we can eat it?" Eddie asked.

"Sure, we can eat these pieces," said Sidney. "There isn't a thing the matter with them. They're just broken, instead of cut."

"Well, O.K.," said Eddie, "and thanks for helping me."

"Good-bye!" Sidney called, as Eddie set off with his express wagon toward the kitchen door.

When Eddie showed his mother what had happened, she did all she could to comfort him. "Sid thinks I can take these pieces to school," said Eddie. "We can still have a watermelon party, but the pieces will be awful little."

"Well, everyone will know that it was a very big watermelon," said his mother.

"Do you think there is enough left for me to get a Green Thumb Award?" Eddie asked.

"I'm sure there is," his mother replied, putting the pieces into the refrigerator.

When all of the pieces were stowed away, Eddie said, "I have to go to the library now."

"You can drive over with me," said his mother. "I have some errands to do. Wait for me and I'll bring you back."

"Swell!" said Eddie. "I like to read in the library."

In a little while Mrs. Wilson was ready to leave. Eddie had his books. He climbed into the car beside his mother and they were off.

They had been gone about five minutes when Rudy and the twins came home. "Let's see if there's anything to eat," said Joe.

"Yes," said Frank. "Let's see what's in the refrigerator."

"I'd like something nice and juicy," said Rudy.

The three boys went into the kitchen. Frank opened the refrigerator door. "Oh, boys!" he cried. "Look at all that watermelon!"

"Watermelon!" cried Rudy. "That's for me!"

"Do you think Mum will mind if we eat it?" said Joe.

"Oh, no," replied Frank. "You know she always says, 'Eat all the fruit you want. It's good for you!' "

"It's all in pieces anyway," said Rudy, helping himself to a large piece.

"I'm going to sit on the back steps and eat mine," said Frank.

"That's a good place," said Rudy, "right by the garbage can." The boys laughed as they sat down on the steps.

"This is the best watermelon I ever ate," said Joe, as he went back for a second piece.

"Bring me another piece," Frank called out. "It's super!"

"I wonder how Eddie's watermelon is coming along," said Rudy, taking a big juicy bite.

"It should be ready to pick soon," said Frank. "It sure is a prize watermelon."

When Frank went back for another piece,

Rudy said, "Leave a piece for Dad. He likes watermelon."

"There are a couple of hunks left," said Frank, returning with three more pieces.

Just then Sidney came running to the steps. "Where's Eddie?" she said.

"I guess he went out," replied Joe. "I haven't seen him."

"We're having a watermelon feast," said Rudy. "Come have a piece."

A look of horror spread over Sidney's face. She looked at Eddie's brothers. She looked from one to another with her hand over her mouth. Then she stammered, "That—that isn't—that isn't Eddie's watermelon, is it?"

"What do you mean, Eddie's watermelon?" said Rudy.

"Why, you know," replied Sidney. "Eddie's prize watermelon that he's been growing."

"Don't be silly," said Joe. "How could Eddie's watermelon be in the refrigerator, all in pieces?"

"Because he dropped it," said Sidney. "It smashed into pieces, but he was going to take the pieces to school to get his Green Thumb Award."

Suddenly the boys had had enough watermelon. "What shall we do?" exclaimed Frank. Before anyone could answer his question, Mrs. Wilson and Eddie drove into the driveway. Without a word, Sidney ran home. "You're the oldest, Rudy," said Frank, "you tell them."

"Well, you fellows stay right here," said Rudy. "Right here beside me."

Rudy, with a twin on each side, walked to meet their mother and Eddie. It only took a moment to tell the sad story. Eddie was furious. "My watermelon!" he cried. "My prize watermelon! Now I won't get a Green Thumb Award!" Eddie ran to the garbage can and lifted the lid. "Look at it!" he cried. "My watermelon! Just garbage! I can't take the garbage can to school. I can't get a Green Thumb Award for a lot of garbage."

The boys told Eddie, over and over, how sorry they were. "We wouldn't have done it on purpose," said Frank.

"We'll buy you a watermelon," said Joe. "A big one."

"A bought watermelon won't get me a Green Thumb Award," said Eddie.

At last Eddie quieted down. He even agreed to eat a piece of his watermelon. "I feel as though I'm eating a pet," said Eddie. This made Eddie remember that he had not fed his rabbits. As soon as he had finished eating the watermelon, he said, "I'm going to feed my rabbits."

On his way to the rabbit hutch Eddie met Sidney. He was surprised to see that she was carrying the leopard skin from her scare-rabbit. "Eddie," said Sidney, holding it out to him, "I would like to give you this. It's sort of beat up 'cause it's been out in the rain and everything, but if you brush it, I think it will look better."

"But that's your scarerabbit, Sid!" said Eddie. "You don't want to give up your scare-rabbit!"

"Oh, that's all right," said Sidney. "I don't need a scarerabbit now. I thought maybe you might like it."

"Oh, Sid," said Eddie. "You know that this is very valuable property. Are you sure you don't want to keep it?"

"No, I really don't want it anymore," said Sidney. "I would like you to have it, Eddie."

Eddie was speechless. He just stammered, "That's swell, Sid! Thanks! Just hold it for me while I feed my rabbits."

"I'll hold it behind my back," said Sidney. "I wouldn't want to scare your rabbits."

When Eddie finished feeding his rabbits, Sidney handed the leopard skin to him. "Thanks, Sid!" Eddie said. "It's swell of you to give me this!"

"I'll see you in school tomorrow," said Sidney.

"What are you going to take for the vegetable show?" Eddie asked.

"Oh, just a bunch of my parsley," said Sidney.

"Well, tie it up with Christmas ribbon, Sid," said Eddie. "It will look great."

Sidney laughed. "How many days are there until Christmas now, Eddie?" she asked.

"I don't know," said Eddie, "but you sure are a Santa Claus, to give me this valuable property!"

When Eddie went to bed he did not go to sleep right away. He was trying to think of something that he could take to school for the vegetable show. He thought and he thought.

Finally he had an idea. While he was thinking about it, he fell asleep.

When Eddie arrived at school the next morning, he was pulling his express wagon. In the wagon there was a box. "Is that your watermelon?" asked Anna Patricia, running up to Eddie. Before Eddie could reply Anna Patricia looked into the box. There she saw Eddie's three rabbits. "Where's your watermelon?" Anna Patricia asked in surprise.

Eddie told the long story about the watermelon to Anna Patricia. "Oh, Eddie! How terrible! I'm so sorry!" said Anna Patricia.

"I brought my rabbits instead," said Eddie.

"But rabbits don't grow in a vegetable garden," said Anna Patricia.

"Well, these rabbits did," said Eddie. "They were born right in my garden, and I raised them on vegetables that I grew."

Eddie took his rabbits into the school. During the morning the children did a good bit of talking about Eddie's rabbits. "I don't think anybody should get a Green Thumb Award for raising rabbits," said Alex. "You wouldn't give anyone a Green Thumb Award for raising bugs."

"I think he should have a Green Paw Award!" said Sidney. All of the children laughed.

"That's right, Mrs. Bolling!" said Boodles. "May I say, 'All in favor?' "

"Yes, you may," said Mrs. Bolling.

Boodles stood up, and said, "All in favor of giving Eddie a Green Paw Award, please say *aye!"* All of the children voted in favor of giving Eddie this unexpected award.

That evening the Wilson family was gathered in their living room. It was a cool evening. Mrs. Wilson buttoned her sweater, and said, "I believe we would enjoy a fire in the fireplace."

"I'll get some wood," said Rudy.

"I'll open the damper," said Eddie. Eddie knelt down beside the fireplace. He put his hand in and took hold of the handle of the damper. He pushed it, and the damper opened. Dried leaves fell into the fireplace. Eddie heard something ring as it hit the brick floor under the chimney. He looked down and there, lying among the leaves, was Eddie's best pencil and a dollar bill.

Eddie picked up the pencil and the dollar

bill, and said, "Hot diggety! Look what's here! Big Boy must have dropped my pencil and our dollar from our vegetable stand down the chimney. I guess they've been lying on the damper all this time."

"By the way," said Eddie's father. "Speaking of vegetables, I forgot to ask how you made out with the Green Thumb Award."

"Oh, they voted to give me the Green Paw Award," replied Eddie.

"Well, you get the Green Thumb Award from me," said his father. "We had the best vegetables I have ever eaten, and they all came out of your garden."

"Thanks, Dad," said Eddie, looking at his thumb. "It's awful dirty. Maybe it would really look green if I washed the dirt off."

His mother laughed. "Try it, Eddie!" she said. "It would be a nice change."

CAROLYN HAYWOOD is distinguished both as author and illustrator of children's books. Her first book was published in 1939. Since then she has had twenty-four other books published and has become one of the most widely read American writers for younger children.

Carolyn Haywood was born in Philadelphia and still lives in that city. She is a graduate of the Philadelphia Normal School and studied at the Pennsylvania Academy of Fine Arts, where she won the Cresson European Scholarship for distinguished work. Miss Haywood calls herself a "grand-pupil" of the great American illustrator, Howard Pyle, having studied with three of his distinguished pupils, Elizabeth Shippen Elliott, Violet Oakley, and Jessie Willcox Smith. She is also a portrait painter and has specialized in portraits of children. Her experience in this field has given her a sympathetic understanding of children and their interests, which has made her peculiarly well fitted to write and illustrate for them. She is continuing her portrait work with commissions in New York, Philadelphia, and other eastern cities.